THE WOMAN WITH THE VELVET NECKLACE.

Comtesse du Barry.

THE WOMAN WITH THE VELVET NECKLACE

BY
ALEXANDRE DUMAS.

Fredonia Books
Amsterdam, The Netherlands

The Woman with the Velvet Necklace

by
Alexandre Dumas

ISBN: 1-4101-0048-0

Reprinted from the 1898 edition

Fredonia Books
Amsterdam, The Netherlands
http://www.fredoniabooks.com

In order to make original editions of historical works available to scholars at an economical price, this facsimile of the original edition of 1898 is reproduced from the best available copy and has been digitally enhanced to improve legibility, but the text remains unaltered to retain historical authenticity.

INTRODUCTORY NOTE.

THE WOMAN WITH THE VELVET NECKLACE.

THE weird and fanciful episode of which Dumas has made Ernst Theodor Wilhelm Hoffmann the hero is in Hoffmann's own peculiar vein, and might well have been a conceit of the gifted German himself, "who is chiefly celebrated," says Dr. Hedge, "for his successful use of the magic and demoniac element in fiction."

Hoffmann was, as we are told by Dumas, born at Königsberg in 1776. He was educated for the bar, and during his early manhood held several minor judicial offices in Posen and Warsaw. In 1816 he became a councillor in the Royal Court at Berlin. He died in 1822, at the early age of forty-six, his constitution having been undermined by dissipation. His father, a man of bad temper, deserted him in his childhood and his uncle, a pedant, educated him. The combination of his father's temper, which he inherited, and of his uncle's habits, which he acquired, resulted in a mental unnaturalness and unsoundness which he never outgrew. In his early manhood he lost his position as a result of Napoleon's invasion, and for several years earned his living by giving lessons in music and drawing, two arts of which he was a perfect master. When he was reinstated in his office, he evinced an irritability of temper and had contracted habits which unfitted him for respectable society. He retired from the drawing-room to the tavern, where his keen wit and brilliant imagination soon gathered a coterie of revellers about him. His mind exhibited, according to Menzel, a curious combination of manliness, humor, poetry, and morbid sensibility. "From the devil down to a wry-faced child's doll, from the dissonance of life which rends the soul, down to a dissonance in music which only rends the ear, the immeasurable kingdom of the ugly and the repulsive was gathered about him, and his descriptions paint alternately these tormenting objects and the torments they prepare for a beautiful soul, with inimitable vividness and truth. . . . Hoffmann's innermost being was music; and the prayer of St. Anthony is never wanting to his hellish caricatures, nor the Christmas bell to his witches' sabbath." He was a very prolific writer, principally of short tales.

Frederick Ludwig Zacharias Werner attained eminence principally as a dramatist. He was born at Königsberg in 1768, and was therefore eight years older than Hoffmann. He became a Roman Catholic in 1811 and was ordained a priest in 1814. He preached in Vienna during the Congress of the Powers, and made a tremendous sensation by the blending in his sermons of coarseness and real power. He was in Poland during 1816 and 1817, but in the latter year returned to Vienna, where he continued to preach with great effect until his death in 1823. His *Works*, dramas, lyric poems, hymns, sermons, etc., fill fourteen volumes. Hoffman composed the incidental music for some of his dramas.

Danton's weaknesses are so well known and so important a part of the history of the man and his time that we need cite no evidence in support of the *vraisemblance* of his relations with Arsène. His dissipated habits and his susceptibility to the charms of the other sex did much to neutralize the influence of his very great powers as an orator and a demagogue, to weaken his hold upon even his most devoted adherents, and thereby to hasten his downfall and the triumph of his former colleague and ally, Robespierre. "Danton," says Lamartine, "lacked nothing of being a great man, save virtue."

INTRODUCTORY NOTE.

It is impossible to imagine a more striking and instructive contrast than that presented by the two pictures of Madame du Barry in the two romances contained in this volume. And both, it need hardly be said, are equally true to life. The bearing and conduct on the scaffold of that woman of the people, who had risen from the gutter to the most exalted position in the kingdom, might well have caused men's minds to turn backward to that other day — only fifty-three days earlier — when, "amid the hooting of the mob, on a cold October morning, the daughter of the Cæsars was more sublime, more majestic than upon the throne. Dressed in white, like a ghost, pale as death, with a slight tinge of red on the cheek-bones, her eyes injected, not with tears but with blood, her hair blanched by misfortune, she was, to the very end, calm, serene, magnanimous, looking down with a sweet pitying expression upon the infernal tumult that surrounded her."[1]

Speaking of the conduct of Madame du Barry after her condemnation, and after the failure of her frantic, dastardly struggles to obtain pardon, or even a respite, by revealing the hiding-places of all her valuables, and by betraying, giving over to certain death, those whose lives were endangered solely by their devotion to her, the brothers De Goncourt say : —

"It was a time when courage was no longer of any sex. Condemned like men, women died like

[1] Imbert de Saint-Amand: "Les Dernières Années de Louis XV."

men. One would have said they were jealous of the right to die. Some mounted the scaffold as if to the sacrifice, others as if it were the pulpit. Some seemed to be marching forward to posterity, others to a new fatherland. Each was worthy of all. Bourgeoises died like Roman matrons, great ladies died like great noblemen, queens died like kings. But all had the force of an idea, a principle, a faith, a duty, a right, a passion, an illusion, — something in short that sustains the soul and enables it to face death. Madame du Barry had nothing of the sort to enable her to die ; and if there is in her story a scandal that should be forgiven her, it is the scandal of a death that moved the heart of the Terror.

"As she mounted the tumbril, Madame du Barry, to whom at the time of her confession Denisot the magistrate had held out vague hopes of pardon, and who, although her hair had been cut off, did not believe that she was going to die, — Madame du Barry became as white as the dress she wore.

"The mob — a Sunday mob — was awaiting the unhappy woman. And in the front ranks the prisoner could see Greive, who said that evening: 'I never laughed so much in my life as I did when I saw the wry faces that pretty —— made because she was going to die.'

"The horses moved forward slowly.

"The people crowded around to look at the *ci-devant tyrant's harlot*.

"She at whom they gazed saw nothing, heard nothing; she did naught but sigh and sob and choke. . . .

"Suddenly, at the Barrière des Sergents near the Palais-Royal, she raised her eyes as she was passing a milliner's shop where the girls had assembled on the balcony to see, for the last time, her who had been Madame du Barry: it was the shop where she had once been a milliner's apprentice.

. . . . . .

"The executioner and his assistants had difficulty in holding her, in keeping her upon the tumbril, for the convulsions of terror made her struggle to throw herself to the ground.

"These violent struggles, these shrieks were succeeded by entreaties mingled with tears; and the woman, brushing back her short hair from her brow and her eyes, leaned out over the mob, hungering to witness her death, and exclaimed: 'My friends — save me — I never injured any one — in heaven's name, save me!'

"The crowd was amazed. They were so accustomed to see the victims die nobly, die *à la bravade*, that it seemed to them for the first time as if a woman was about to be murdered.

"Meanwhile she exclaimed, still weeping, 'Life! life! — give me my life. I give all my property to the nation!'

"'Your property! why, you only give the nation what belongs to it already.'

"A charcoal-burner who was standing in front of the scoffer turned, and, without a word, struck him in the face.

"Throughout the silent, stupefied groups there

was that first thrill of emotion which is, in a multitude, a sort of shudder of compassion.

"The driver whipped up his horses and abridged the spectacle.

"The tumbril arrived on Place de la Révolution at half-past four in the afternoon.

"Madame du Barry alighted first. On the steps leading to the scaffold, desperate, mad with anguish and terror, she struggled, implored, begged the executioner for mercy: 'Just one minute more, Monsieur le Bourreau!' and then, as the knife descended: 'Help! help!' like a woman murdered by thieves."[1]

Saint-Amand puts the following words in the mouth of Madame du Barry, speaking from the grave in her turn as the last of the mistresses of Louis XV:—

"'I paid dear for the joys of luxury and a life of licentiousness; I knew not how to live nor to die. At a time when heroism was a commonplace quality I was weak and afraid, I shuddered on the scaffold!'"

The early chapters of "The Woman with the Velvet Necklace," and of "Monsieur de Chauvelin's Will" as well, afford an excellent illustration of the accuracy of the statement made by M. Blaze de Bury in his book upon the works of the elder Dumas. He says that Dumas has told the story of the most important events of his life in his books, and has thereby obviated the necessity of a biography.

[1] E. & J. de Goncourt: "La du Barry."

INTRODUCTORY NOTE.

Charles Nodier was one of the dearest of the many dear friends who did homage to the many lovable qualities of the great romancist, and this is not the only one of Dumas' works in which he has taken occasion to express his appreciation of the friendship and kindness of that accomplished, versatile, and prolific man of letters, and discoverer of the taratantaleo.

The story of Dumas' first acquaintance with Monsieur de Villenave and with Nodier is told by him in substantially the same form, but with somewhat more detail, in the fifth volume of "Mes Mémoires."

CONTENTS.

———◆———

CONTENTS.

LIST OF CHARACTERS.

Period, 1793.

———◆———

ERNST THEODOR WILHELM HOFFMANN.

SOPHIA, his aunt.

ZACHARIAS WERNER, his friend.

GOTTLIEB MURR, leader of the orchestra at the Mannheim
Theatre.

ANTONIA, his daughter.

DANTON.

ROBESPIERRE.

COMTESSE DU BARRY.

CITIZEN FOUQUIER, public prosecutor at Paris.

AN EXECUTIONER.

THE LANDLADY OF THE QUAI AUX FLEURS.

MONSIEUR VESTRIS, of the Théâtre de la Porte Saint-Martin.

ARSÈNE, a danseuse, mistress of Danton.

EUCHARIS, her maid.

THE PHYSICIAN TO THE OPÉRA AT THE PORTE SAINT-MARTIN
THEATRE.

THE WOMAN WITH THE VELVET NECKLACE.

I.

THE ARSENAL.

On the 4th of December, 1846, my vessel having cast anchor on the preceding day in the Bay of Tunis, I awoke about five o'clock in the morning, conscious of one of those lowering clouds of profound melancholy which keep the eye moist and the breast swollen for a whole day.

That feeling was the result of a dream.

I jumped out of my bunk, I drew on a pair of trousers with feet, I went on deck, and I looked about me.

I hoped that the marvellous landscape that was exposed to my gaze would relieve my mind from its preoccupation, which was the more obstinate for the very reason that it had no real cause.

I had in front of me, within gunshot, the jetty extending from the Goletta fort to the fort of the Arsenal, leaving a narrow passage for vessels which desire to go from the gulf into the lake. This lake, whose waters are as blue as the azure of the heavens they reflect, was ruffled in certain places by the flapping wings of a flock of swans, while, upon stakes

1

planted at intervals to indicate shoal places, stood an occasional cormorant, perfectly motionless, like the birds we see carved on sepulchres. Suddenly he would let himself fall like a stone, dive for his prey, return to the surface with a fish in his beak, swallow the fish, remount his stake, and resume his silent immobility until another fish, passing within range, tempted his appetite, and, overcoming his indolence, caused him to disappear and reappear once more.

Meanwhile, at intervals of five minutes, the air would be streaked by a long file of flamingoes, whose diamond-shaped purple wings showed dark against the dull white of their bodies, and made them resemble a pack of cards composed entirely of aces of diamonds flying through the air in a single line.

On the horizon was Tunis, that is to say, a mass of square houses, without windows or openings of any sort, arranged like the seats of an amphitheatre, white as chalk, and outlined against the sky with extraordinary sharpness. On the left, like a vast crenellated wall, rose the Lead Mountains, whose name indicates their sombre color. At their feet crouched the mosque and village of Sidi-Fathallah. On the right could be distinguished the tomb of Saint-Louis and the spot where Carthage was, two of the grandest memorials in the history of the world. Astern of us the Montezuma rode at anchor, a magnificent steam frigate, with engines of four hundred and fifty horse power.

Certainly there was enough to divert the most pre-occupied imagination. At sight of all that wealth of beauty one might well have forgotten yesterday, to-day, and to-morrow. But my mind was ten years away, fixed obstinately upon a single thought which a dream had nailed in my brain.

My eye became fixed on vacancy. All that magnificent panorama gradually faded away as my gaze grew more and more vague. Soon I had ceased to see everything that really existed. Reality disappeared, and amid that misty void, as if beneath a fairy's wand, appeared a salon with white wainscoting, and in a recess, seated at a piano over which her fingers wandered carelessly, was a woman, at once inspired and pensive, a muse and a saint. I recognized that woman, and I murmured as if she could hear me, —

"I salute you, Marie, full of grace. My mind is with you."

And then, no longer trying to resist that white-winged angel who, like a beautiful vision, carrying me back to the days of my youth, revealed to me the pure features of that maiden, young wife, and mother, I yielded to the current of the stream called memory, which flows back to the past instead of flowing onward to the future.

Thereupon I was seized by that selfish impulse — selfish and consequently natural to man — which impels him not to keep a thought to himself, but to double the scope of his feelings by communicating them, and to pour into another heart the fluid, be it sweet or bitter, with which his own is filled.

I took a pen and I wrote, —

"ON BOARD THE VÉLOCE, IN SIGHT OF CARTHAGE AND TUNIS.
December 4, 1846.

"MADAME, — Upon opening a letter dated from Carthage and Tunis, you will wonder who can have written to you from such a spot, and you will hope perhaps to receive an autograph of Regulus or Louis IX. Alas! madame, he who from so great a distance lays his humble souvenir at your feet is neither a hero nor a saint, and if he has ever shown any resemblance to the Bishop of Hippone, whose tomb he visited three days since, that resemblance can be applicable only to the first part of that great man's life. It is true that, like him, he may redeem that first part of his life by the second. But it is very late already to do penance, and, in all probability, he will die as he has lived, not daring even to leave his confessions behind him, for while they might possibly bear being told, they could hardly be read.

"You have already turned to the signature, have you not, madame, and you know whom you have to deal with; so that now you are asking yourself how it happened that the author of 'Monte Cristo' and 'Les Mousquetaires,' standing between this magnificent lake which is the grave of a city and the poor monument which is a king's sepulchre, thought of writing to you, — to you, when at Paris, at your very door, he sometimes does not call upon you for a whole year at a time.

"In the first place, madame, Paris is Paris, that is to say, a sort of whirlpool, where one loses the memory of everything amid the noise that the people make in running to and fro, and the earth in revolving. At Paris, you see, I do as the rest of the world and the earth do; I run to and fro and revolve, to say nothing of the fact that, when I am neither running nor revolving, I am writing. But then, madame, it is a different matter, and when I am writing I am not so entirely apart from you as you think, for you are one of the few persons for whom I write, and it is a very unusual thing, if I do not say to myself when I finish a chapter that pleases me, or a book that is well received, 'Marie Nodier, that creature of rare and charming mind, will read that;' and I am proud when I say it, madame, for I hope that after you have read what I have written, I may perhaps grow a little taller in your mind.

"But to return to my thought, madame: I dreamed last night of you, forgetting the swell that rolled beneath a huge steam vessel which the government has loaned me, and upon which I am entertaining one of your friends and one of your admirers, Boulanger and my son, not to mention Giraud, Maquet, Chancel, and Desbarolles, who are included among your acquaintances; as I was saying, I fell asleep, thinking of nothing in particular, and as I am almost always in the land of the Thousand and One Nights, a genie visited me and led me into a dream of which you were the queen. The place to which he took me, or rather took me back, madame, was much better than a palace, was much better than a kingdom; it was that kindly, excellent household at the Arsenal in the days of its happiness and joy, when our beloved Charles did the honors with all the freedom of ancient hospitality and our highly respected Marie with all the charm of modern hospitality.

"Ah! madame, be sure that when I wrote those lines I uttered a heartfelt sigh. Those were happy times for me. Your charming wit inspired everybody, and sometimes, I venture to say, myself more than anybody else. You see that it is an egotistical sentiment that leads me to address you. I borrowed something of your adorable gayety, as the pebble of the poet Saadi borrowed a portion of the rose's perfume.

"Do you remember Paul's archer's costume? Do you remember Francisque Michel's yellow shoes? Do you remember my son as a waterman? Do you remember the recess where the piano was and where you sang "Lazzara," that wonderful melody which you promised me, and which, be it said without reproach, you never gave me?

"As I am appealing to your memory, let us go still further: do you remember Fontaney and Alfred Johannot, those two veiled figures who always maintained their melancholy demeanor amid our laughter, for there is a vague foreboding of the tomb in men who are destined to die young. Do you remember Taylor sitting in a corner, motionless and dumb, wondering what new voyage he could undertake, to enrich France with a Spanish painting, a Greek bas-relief, or an Egyptian obelisk? Do you remember De Vigny, who at that time suspected his coming transfiguration perhaps, and disdained to mingle with the common herd of men? Do you remember Lamartine, standing in front of the fire and tossing the harmony of his noble lines at our feet? Do you remember Hugo, looking at him and listening to him as Eteocles must have looked at and listened to Polynice, the only one among us with the smile of equality upon his lips, while Madame Hugo, playing with her lovely hair, half reclined on the couch, as if fatigued by the share of glory that fell to her lot?

"And then, in the midst of it all, your mother, so simple and kindly and sweet; your aunt, Madame de Tercy, so witty and good-humored; Dauzats, so fanciful and turgid and enthusiastic; Barye, so alone amid the noise, that it always seemed as if his thought was sent by his body in search of one of the seven wonders of the world; Boulanger, to-day so depressed, to-morrow so cheerful, always such a great painter and poet, always so true a friend in his times of cheerfulness and of depression alike; and lastly the little girl gliding about among the poets, painters, musicians, great men, men of intellect and scholars; the little girl whom I used to take in the hollow of my hand and offer to you as if she were a statuette by Barre or by Pradier! Ah! *Mon Dieu!* what has become of them all, madame?

"The Lord breathed upon the keystone of the arch and the magic edifice crumbled, and those who were within fled, and the very spot where everything was alive and blooming and flourishing is now a desert.

"Fontaney and Alfred Johannot are dead, Taylor has given up travelling, De Vigny has withdrawn from sight, Lamartine is a deputy, Hugo a peer of France, and Boulanger, my son, and myself are at Carthage, whence I look toward you, madame, as I heave the heartfelt sigh I mentioned just now, which, despite the wind that whirls away like a cloud the dying smoke of our vessel, will not overtake those cherished memories which dark-winged time silently enwraps in the grayish mist of the past.

"O springtime, youth of the year! O youth, springtime of life!

"Ah, well! that is the vanished world that my dream brought back to me last night, as bright and visible, but alas! at the same time as impalpable as the atoms that dance in the sunbeam that creeps into a dark room through a chink in the shutter.

"And now, madame, you are no longer surprised at this letter, are you? The present would capsize constantly were it not held in equilibrium by the weight of hope and the counterpoise of memory, and, it may be luckily or unluckily, I am one of those in whom memory is stronger than hope.

"Now let us talk of something else; for while we may be permitted to be sad, it is only on condition that we do not darken the lives of others with our melancholy. What is my friend Boniface doing? Eight or ten days ago I visited a town which will cause him many a weary hour when he finds its name in the pages of that base usurer whom we call Sallust. That town is Constantine, the ancient Cyrta, a marvel of architecture built on the summit of a rock, by a race of fantastic animals, I doubt not, with the wings of an eagle and human hands, such as Herodotus and Levaillant, those two great travellers, saw and described.

"Then we passed a little time at Utica and much at Biserta. Giraud made a portrait of a Turkish notary in the latter city, and Boulanger of his chief clerk. I send them to you, madame, so that you may compare them with the notaries and chief clerks of Paris. I doubt whether the result will be favorable to the latter.

"I fell into the water while hunting flamingoes and swans, an accident that might have had unpleasant results in the Seine, which is probably frozen solid at this moment, but in Cato's Lake it was inconvenient simply because it made me take a bath with my clothes on, to the great astonishment of Alexandre, Giraud, and the governor of the town, who were following our boat with their eyes from a terrace, and could not understand an occurrence which they attributed to a mental vagary on my part, whereas it was due to the displacement of my centre of gravity.

"I emerged from the water like the cormorants I mentioned just now, madame; like them I disappeared, like them I returned to the surface! but I had not, as they had, a fish in my beak.

"Five minutes after it happened I had forgottten all about it, and was as dry as Monsieur Valéry, the sun was so obliging in its attentions.

"Oh! I would that I could guide a beam of this lovely sunlight to you, madame, wherever you may be, were it only to make a sprig of myosotis bloom upon your window-sill.

"Adieu, madame; forgive this long letter. I am not in the habit of doing such things, and, like the child who was defending himself against the charge of having made the world, I promise you that I will not do it again; but why did the concierge of heaven leave open the ivory gate through which golden dreams come forth?

"Please to accept, madame, the homage of my most respectful sentiments.

"ALEXANDRE DUMAS.

"I press Jules' hand warmly."

Why do I quote that essentially private letter? Because before telling my readers the story of the woman with the velvet necklace, it was necessary for me to throw open to them the doors of the Arsenal, that is to say of the home of Charles Nodier.

And now that that door has been opened by the hand of his daughter, and we are therefore sure of a welcome, "Let him who loves me follow me."

At the farther end of Paris stands a large building of gloomy and forbidding appearance, called the Arsenal, a sort of continuation of the Quai des Célestins, overlooking the river, and with Rue Morland at its rear.

A part of the ground on which that substantial edifice is built was called, before the city moats were dug, the Champ-au-Plâtre. Paris, one day when preparations for war were in progress, purchased the field and built sheds there to house its artillery. About 1533 François I. discovered that he was in need of cannon, and conceived the idea of having them cast for himself. So he borrowed one of the sheds from his faithful city, promising of course to restore it as soon as the casting was completed. Then, on the pretext of hastening the work, he borrowed another, and then a third, always with the same promise; but in the end, acting upon the principle that what is worth taking is worth keeping, he unceremoniously kept the three buildings he had borrowed.

Twenty years later about twenty thousand pounds of powder that were stored there took fire. There was a terrific explosion. Paris trembled as Catania trembles on the days when Enceladus changes his position. Stones were hurled as far as Faubourg Saint-Marceau. The roaring of the terrible thunder caused a commotion at Melun. The houses in the vicinity wavered for a moment as if they were drunk, then fell in. Fish died in the river, killed by the sudden shock, and thirty people, who were blown into the air by the hurricane of flame, fell to the ground in thousands of pieces; a hundred and fifty were wounded. How did the horrible thing happen? What was the cause of the disaster? No one ever knew, and in view of the general ignorance, it was imputed to the Protestants.

Charles IX. caused the buildings to be rebuilt on a more extensive scale. A great builder was Charles IX. The gallery of the Louvre was built under his auspices, and the Innocents' fountain hewn by Jean Goujon, who was killed there by a spent ball, as every one knows. The great artist and great poet would certainly have completed the work, had not God, who had certain questions to ask him on the subject of August 24, 1572, summoned him.

His successors resumed the construction of the buildings where he had left it, and went on with it. In

1584, under Henri III., the doorway facing the Quai des Célestins, was carved. It was flanked by pillars in the shape of cannon, and on the marble shelf above could be read this distich of Nicolas Bourbon, which Santeuil sought to purchase at the price of the scaffold: —

> " Ætna hic Henrico vulcania tela ministrat,
>   Tela giganteos debellatura furores ; — "

Which may be translated thus: —

" Ætna forges here the shafts with which Henri will overwhelm the savage fury of the giants."

And, in truth, after crushing the giants of the League, Henri laid out the lovely garden which we see on the maps of the time of Louis XIII., while Sully established his ministerial quarters there, and presided at the painting and gilding of the beautiful salons which today form the library of the Arsenal.

In 1823 Charles Nodier was chosen director of that library, and left Rue de Choiseul, where he then lived, to take up his abode in his new quarters.

A most delightful man was Nodier. Without a vice, but full of faults, those fascinating faults in which the originality of a man of genius consists, lavish, heedless, and an idler, — an idler as Figaro was indolent, with hearty enjoyment.

Nodier knew almost everything that it is given to man to know. Moreover, Nodier had the privilege of the man of genius. When he did not know he invented, and what he invented was far more ingenious, more highly colored, more probable than the reality.

Moreover, though full of systems, and an enthusiastic dealer in paradoxes, Nodier was in no sense a propagandist, and it was for his own amusement only that he was paradoxical, for himself only that he constructed systems. If his systems were adopted and his paradoxes understood, he immediately varied them and set about making others.

Nodier was like the man in Terence to whom nothing human was without interest. He loved for the sake of loving. He loved as the sun shines, as the brook murmurs, as the flower gives perfume. Whatever was good, whatever was beautiful, whatever was great appealed to his sympathies. Even in evil he sought what there was of good, just as the chemist extracts a salutary medicine from the poisonous plant, from the heart of the very poison itself.

How many times had Nodier been in love? It would have been impossible for him to answer the question himself. Moreover, great poet that he was, he constantly confounded dreams with realities. Nodier had so fondly caressed the caprices of his imagination that he had come at last to believe in their existence. To him " Thérèse Aubert," the " Fée aux Miettes," and " Inès de la Sierra " were real persons. They were his daughters as Marie was. They were Marie's sisters, only Madame Nodier had had no part in their creation. Like Jupiter, Nodier had evolved all those Minervas from his brain.

But not human beings alone, not Eve's daughter and Adam's sons alone did Nodier animate with his life-giving breath. Nodier had invented an animal and christened it. He had then, on his own authority, without concerning himself as to what God would say, endowed it with immortality.

That animal was the tarantaleo.

You do not know the tarantaleo, do you? Nor do I; but Nodier knew it, knew it by heart. He would describe to you the taratantaleo's manners and customs and caprices. He would have told you of its love affairs, if, from the moment he discovered that the taratantaleo bore within him the principle of everlasting life, he had not condemned him to celibacy, reproduction being useless where resurrection exists.

How had Nodier discovered the taratantaleo?

I am about to tell you.

At eighteen years of age Nodier was interested in entomology. Nodier's life was divided into six different phases: —

First he devoted himself to natural history: " La Bibliothèque Entomologique."

Then to philology: " Le Dictionnaire des Onomatopées."

Then to politics: " La Napoleone."

Then to religious philosophy: " Les Méditations du Cloître."

Then to poetry: " Les Essais d'un Jeune Barde."

Then to novel-writing: " Jean Sbogar," " Smarra," " Trilby," " Le Peintre de Salzbourg," " Mademoiselle de Marsan," " Adèle," " Le Vampire," " Le Songe d'Or," " Les Souvenirs de Jeunesse," " Le Roi de Bohème et ses Sept Châteaux," " Les Fantaisies du Docteur Néophobus," and a thousand other delightful things which you know, which I know, but whose names do not come to my pen.

Nodier then was in the first phase of his labors. He was engaged in the study of entomology, and lived on the sixth floor, one floor higher than the poet Béranger. He was making experiments upon infinitely small creatures under the microscope, and he discovered a whole world of invisible animalculæ long before Raspail. One day, after subjecting to a careful scrutiny water, wine, vinegar, cheese, bread, everything in fact upon which experiments are usually made, he picked up a little moist sand from the gutter and placed it on the slide of his microscope, then put his eye to the lens.

Thereupon he saw a strange animal, shaped like a velocipede, moving across the slide, having two wheels which he worked very rapidly. Had he a stream to cross? His wheels served the same purpose as the paddle-wheels of a steamboat. Had he a tract of dry land to cross? His wheels served the same purpose as the wheels of a cab. Nodier watched him, dissected him, sketched him, and analyzed him for so long a time that, suddenly remembering that he had an appointment, he hurried away, leaving his microscope, his grain of sand, and the taratantaleo, whose world it was.

When Nodier returned home it was late. He was tired, so he went to bed and slept as one sleeps at eighteen. Not until he opened his eyes the next morning, therefore, did he think of his grain of sand, his microscope, and his taratantaleo.

Alas! during the night the sand had dried and the poor taratantaleo, which undoubtedly required some dampness to support life, was dead. His tiny body lay on its side, the wheels were motionless. The steamboat no longer moved, the velocipede had stopped.

But, dead as he was, the animal was none the less an interesting variety of the *ephemera*, and his corpse was as well worth preserving as that of a mammoth or a mastodon; but, as you will see, it was necessary to take vastly greater precautions to handle a creature a hundred times smaller than a flesh-worm, than to move an animal ten times larger than an elephant.

Nodier used the point of a pen, therefore, to transport

the grain of sand from the slide of the microscope to a small pasteboard box, destined to be the taratantaleo's sepulchre.

He promised himself that he would show the body to the first scientist who should venture to climb up his six flights of stairs.

There are so many things for a youth of eighteen to think about, that he may be forgiven for forgetting the dead body of an ephemeral insect. Nodier forgot the taratantaleo's body for three months, six months, perhaps a year.

But one day he happened to notice the box. He was desirous to see what change a year had produced in the animal. It was a cloudy day and the rain was falling heavily. In order to see better, he went to the window and emptied the contents of the little box onto the slide of his microcsope.

The body was still lying on the sand motionless; but time, which has so great an effect upon larger creatures, seemed to have overlooked the infinitely small.

Nodier was looking at his treasure, when suddenly a drop of rain, driven by the wind, fell upon the slide of the microscope and moistened the grain of sand.

Thereupon, at the first touch of that revivifying moisture, it seemed to Nodier that his taratantaleo came to life again, that he moved one feeler, then another; that he turned one of his wheels; that he turned both wheels; that he recovered his centre of gravity; that his movements became regular; in a word, that he lived.

The miracle of resurrection was accomplished, not after three days, but after a year.

Ten times Nodier repeated the same test. Ten times

the sand dried and the taratantaleo died. Ten times
the sand was moistened, and ten times the taratantaleo
came to life.

It was not one of the *ephemera* which Nodier had
discovered, but an immortal. In all probability his
taratantaleo had seen the Deluge and was destined to
be present at the Last Judgment.

Unluckily, one day when Nodier was preparing, perhaps for the twentieth time, to repeat his experiment, a
gust of wind carried away the dry grain of sand, and
with it the corpse of the phenomenal taratantaleo.

Nodier picked up many grains of moist sand from
his gutter and elsewhere, but it was of no avail. He
never found the duplicate of what he had lost. The
taratantaleo was the only one of his kind, and, lost to
mankind, he lived only in Nodier's memory. But he
lived there in such a way as never to be effaced.

We have spoken of Nodier's faults. His dominant
fault, in Madame Nodier's eyes at least, was his biblio-
mania. That fault, which was Nodier's joy, drove
his wife to despair.

The difficulty was that all the money Nodier earned
went for books. How many times, when he had gone
out to collect two or three hundred francs that were
absolutely necessary for the household expenses, did he
return home with a rare volume, an only copy!

The money had stuck fast in the till of Techener or
Guillemot.

Madame Nodier would attempt to scold him. But
Nodier would take his volume from his pocket, open it,
close it, pat it with his hand, point out to his wife an
error in printing that proved the genuineness of the
book, saying, —

"Remember, my dear love, that I can find three

hundred francs another time, while such another book as this, hum! such another book, hum! is not to be found.   Ask Pixérécourt."

Pixérécourt was Nodier's great admiration, for Nodier always adored melodrama.   He called Pixérécourt the Corneille of the boulevards.

Pixérécourt called on Nodier almost every morning. The morning at Nodier's was given over to visits from bibliophiles.   There were wont to assemble the Marquis de Ganay, the Marquis de Château-Giron, the Marquis de Chalabre, the Comte de Labédoyère, Bérard, the man of the Elzevirs, who, in his leisure moments, revised the Charter of 1830, the bibliophile Jacob, the learned Weiss of Besançon, the universal scholar Peignot of Dijon; and all the foreign scholars, who, immediately on their arrival in Paris, procured an introduction or introduced themselves to that circle, whose reputation was European.

There they all consulted Nodier, the oracle of the assemblage.   They showed him books.   They asked him for memoranda concerning them.   It was his favorite amusement.   The scholars of the Institute seldom appeared at those gatherings.   They looked upon Nodier with jealousy.   Nodier combined wit and poetic talent with learning, and that is an offence which the Academy of Sciences is no more ready to pardon than the Académie Française.

And then Nodier often jested and he sometimes bit. One day he wrote "Le Roi de Bohème et ses Sept Châteaux."   That time he carried the day.   Nodier was supposed to have fallen out forever with the Institute.   Not at all.   The Academy of Timbuctoo brought about Nodier's admission to the Académie Française. Sisters owe something to each other.

After two or three hours of work that was always easy to him, of covering ten or twelve pages of paper about six inches by four, with legible, even handwriting, free from erasures, Nodier would go out.

Once out of the house, Nodier prowled about at random, almost always following the line of the quays, however, but crossing and recrossing the bridges, according to the topographical location of the various bookstalls. From the bookstalls he would go to the shops of the publishers, and thence to the bookbinders.

For Nodier was a connoisseur not only in books but in bindings. The masterpieces of Gaseon under Louis XIII., of Desseuil under Louis XIV., of Pasdeloup under Louis XV., and of Derome under Louis XV. and Louis XVI. were so familiar to him that he could distinguish them with his eyes closed, simply by touching them. It was Nodier who had revived the art of binding, which ceased to be an art under the revolutionary government and the Empire. It was he who encouraged and guided the restorers of the art, the Thouvenins, Bradels, Niedrées, Bozonnets, and Legrands. Thouvenin, dying of consumption, rose from his death-bed to cast one last glance at the bindings he was making for Nodier.

Nodier's peregrinations almost always ended at Crozet's or Techener's, those brothers-in-law, parted by rivalry, between whom his placid personality intervened. There the bibliophiles assembled to discuss books, editions, sales. There they made exchanges. As soon as Nodier appeared there was a shout of welcome; but as soon as he opened his mouth, absolute silence. Thereupon Nodier would talk and give utterance to paradoxes *de omni re scibili et quibusdam aliis.*

In the evening, after the family dinner, Nodier usually worked in the dining-room between three candles arranged in the shape of a triangle, never more, never less. We have told what sort of paper he used and described his handwriting. He always wrote with goose-quills. Nodier had a horror of steel pens, as of all new inventions in general. Gas made him furious; steam exasperated him. He discovered an infallible sign of the speedy end of the world in the destruction of the forests and the exhaustion of the coal mines. In his fierce tirades against progress and civilization, Nodier's impassioned warmth was particularly resplendent and his vehemence overwhelming.

About half-past nine in the evening Nodier went out. Then he did not follow the line of the quays, but the line of the boulevards. He went to the Porte-Saint-Martin, the Ambigu, or the Funambules, preferably the last-named. It was Nodier who deified Debureau. To Nodier's mind there were but three actors in the world, — Debureau, Potier, and Talma. Potier and Talma were dead, but Debureau remained and consoled Nodier for the loss of the other two.

Nodier had seen the "Bœuf Enragé" a hundred times.

Every Sunday Nodier breakfasted with Pixérécourt. There he met his callers, — the bibliophile Jacob, king while Nodier was not there, vice-king when Nodier appeared; the Marquis de Ganay, the Marquis de Chalabre.

The Marquis de Ganay was a fickle-minded, capricious collector, who loved a book as a roué in the days of the Regency loved a woman, simply to possess it; and when he obtained it he was faithful for a month, — not faithful but enthusiastic, — carrying it in his pocket, stopping his friends to show it to them, putting it

under his pillow, and waking up in the middle of the
night and lighting his candle to gloat over it, but never
reading it; always envious of Pixérécourt's books,
which Pixérécourt refused to sell him at any price; and
revenging himself for that refusal by purchasing at
Madame de Castellane's sale an autograph that Pixérécourt had craved for ten years.

"Never mind!" cried Pixérécourt in a rage, "I will
have it."

"What?" asked the Marquis de Ganay.

"Your autograph."

"And when, pray?"

"*Parbleu!* at your death."

And Pixérécourt would have kept his word if the
Marquis de Ganay had not thought it best to survive
him.

As for the Marquis de Chalabre, he had but one
ambition. That was to possess a Bible that nobody
owned, but that ambition was none the less keen. He
tormented Nodier so, urging him to tell him where he
could procure a copy which had no fellow, that Nodier
at last did even better than the marquis desired. He
told him of a copy that did not exist.

The Marquis de Chalabre immediately set out to find
that copy.

Christopher Columbus displayed no more ardor in his
attempts to discover America, Vasco de Gama was not
more persistent in his search for the Indies than the
Marquis de Chalabre in the pursuit of his Bible. But
America actually existed between latitude 70 degrees
north and latitude 53 and 54 degrees south; India
really lay on this and the other side of the Ganges;
whereas the Marquis de Chalabre's Bible was situated
in no latitude, and did not lie on either side of the

Seine. The result was that Vasco de Gama found India, that Christopher Columbus discovered America, but that the marquis sought in vain from north to south and from east to west. He did not find his Bible.

The more fruitless the search the more ardently the Marquis de Chalabre pursued it.

He had offered five hundred francs for it. He had offered a thousand francs. He had offered two thousand, four thousand, ten thousand francs. All the bibliographers were in a terrible pother on the subject of that wretched Bible. They wrote to Germany and to England. No result. They would not have given themselves so much trouble for a note from the Marquis de Chalabre, but they would simply have replied, "There is no such Bible." But a note from Nodier was a very different matter. If Nodier had said, "Such a Bible is in existence," the Bible undoubtedly existed. The pope might be mistaken, but Nodier was infallible.

The search lasted three years. Every Sunday the Marquis de Chalabre said to Nodier as they breakfasted together at Pixérécourt's, —

"By the way, my dear Charles, about that Bible — "

"Well?"

"It can't be found!"

"*Quære et invenies*," Nodier would reply.

And the bibliomaniac would resume his search with renewed ardor, but he found nothing.

At last they brought the Marquis de Chalabre a Bible.

It was not the one mentioned by Nodier, but there was only a year's difference in the date. It was not printed at Kehl, but it was printed at Strasburg, only a league away. It was not a unique copy, it is true;

but the only other one in existence was in a monastery of the Druses in Lebanon. The Marquis de Chalabre carried the Bible to Nodier and asked his opinion.

"*Dame!*" replied Nodier, seeing that the marquis was quite ready to go mad if he had not some Bible, "take this one, my dear friend, as it's impossible to find the other."

The Marquis de Chalabre purchased the Bible for two thousand francs, had it splendidly rebound, and placed it in a special case.

When he died, the Marquis de Chalabre left his library to Mademoiselle Mars. Mademoiselle Mars, who was nothing less than a bibliomaniac, requested Merlin to catalogue all the books belonging to the deceased and have them sold. Merlin, who was the most honest man on earth, called upon Mademoiselle Mars one day with thirty or forty thousand francs in bank-notes in his hand.

He had found them in a sort of portfolio arranged in the magnificent binding of that almost unique Bible.

"Why," I asked Nodier, "did you play that joke on the poor Marquis de Chalabre, you are so little given to practical joking?"

"Because he was ruining himself, my friend, and because he had n't thought of anything else during the three years that he was engaged in the quest for his Bible. At the end of the three years he spent two thousand francs. During the next three he would have spent fifty thousand."

Now that we have shown our beloved Charles as he appeared during the week and on Sunday morning, let us describe him as he was on Sunday from six o'clock in the afternoon until midnight.

How did I make Nodier's acquaintance?

In the same way that everybody else did. He rendered me a service. It was in 1827, and I had just finished "Christine." I knew no one in the departments, no one at the theatre. My official position, instead of being of assistance to me in attaining the Comédie-Française, was a hindrance. I had written, two or three days earlier, this last line, which has been so loudly hissed and so loudly applauded:—

"Eh bien, — j'en ai pitié, mon père: qu'on l'achève!"

Below that line I had written, THE END. There was nothing more for me to do but to read my piece to messieurs the king's actors, and to be accepted or rejected by them.

Unfortunately at that time the management of the Comédie-Française was, like the government of Venice, republican but aristocratic, and not every one who sought gained access to their most serene highnesses the committee.

There was an examiner whose duty it was to read the works of young men who had done nothing as yet, and who, consequently, were not entitled to have their work read by the committee until it had been examined; but the traditions of the drama contained such doleful stories of manuscripts awaiting their turn to be read for one or two, and even three years, that I, being familiar with Dante and Milton, dared not risk being consigned to that purgatory, trembling lest my poor "Christine" should go to increase the number of

"Questi sciaurati che mai non fur vivi."

I had heard Nodier spoken of as the born protector of every unborn poet. I asked Baron Taylor for a line to introduce me to him. He sent it to me. A week later my play was read at the Théâtre-Français, and was almost accepted.

I say almost, because there were in " Christine," considering the time when it was written, that is to say the year of grace 1827, such literary enormities, that messeieurs the king's actors in ordinary dared not accept me on their own authority, but subordinated their opinion to that of Monsieur Picard, the author of " La Petite Ville."

Monsieur Picard was one of the oracles of the time.

Firmin escorted me to Monsieur Picard. Monsieur Picard received me in a library supplied with all the editions of his works and adorned with his bust. He took my manuscript, made an appointment with me for that day week, and dismissed me.

A week later, hour for hour, I presented myself at Monsieur Picard's door. Monsieur Picard evidently expected me; he greeted me with a smile like Rigobert's in " Maison à Vendre."

"Monsieur," he said to me, handing me my manuscript neatly rolled, "have you any means of subsistence ? "

"Yes, monsieur," I replied. "I have a small place in Monsieur le Duc d'Orléans' household."

"Very good! " he said, putting my roll in my hands with much warmth of manner, and taking my hands at the same time, " go back to your desk, my boy."

And delighted at having said a bright thing, he rubbed his hands, indicating with a gesture that my audience was at an end.

I owed an acknowledgment to Nodier none the less. I called at the Arsenal. Nodier received me, as he received every one, with a smile. But there be smiles and smiles, as Molière says.

I may forget Picard's smile some day, but I shall never forget Nodier's.

I was determined to prove to Nodier that I was not so utterly unworthy his patronage as he might think after what Picard had said to me. I left my manuscript with him. The next day I received a delightful letter, which restored all my courage and invited me to the evenings at the Arsenal.

Those evenings at the Arsenal were most charming functions, to which no pen can ever do justice. They were on Sundays, and really began at six o'clock.

At six o'clock the table was set. The regular guests were the founders of the meetings: Cailleux, Taylor, and Francis Wey, whom Nodier loved like a son; then there were generally one or two specially invited guests, and in addition whoever chose to come.

Once you were admitted to that charming household on a footing of intimacy, you dined with Nodier at your own pleasure. There were always two or three covers laid for chance guests. If the number proved to be insufficient, a fourth was added, and a fifth and a sixth. If it was necessary to lengthen the table, it was lengthened. But woe to him who made the thirteenth! He was pitilessly relegated to a small table, unless a fourteenth came and relieved him from his penance.

Nodier had his foibles; he preferred brown bread to white, pewter to silver plate, tallow candles to wax.

No one paid any attention to them except Madame Nodier, who saw that he had what he wanted.

After a year or two I became one of the intimate friends of whom I spoke just now. I was at liberty to call, without warning, at the dinner hour; I was received with joyous shouts that left me in no doubt as to my welcome, and they gave me a seat at table, or rather I took a seat between Madame Nodier and Marie.

After a certain time, what was only a privilege became a vested right. If I arrived late, if they were at table and my place was taken, they apologized to the usurper, my place was given up to me, and, faith! he whom I displaced found a seat where he could.

Nodier maintained that my presence was a stroke of good fortune for him, in that I made it unnecessary for him to talk. But if it was good fortune for him, it certainly was ill fortune for the others. Nodier was the most delightful talker that ever lived. It was of no use to do to my conversation all that you do to a fire to make it blaze, blow it and poke it and throw on the steel filings that make the mind give forth sparks like those of the forge; there was *verve*, energy, youth, but there was not that kindly wit, that inexpressible charm, that infinite grace in which, as in a snare, the birdcatcher captures all sorts of birds, large and small alike. In a word, I was not Nodier.

I was a makeshift with which they had to be content, that was all.

But sometimes I sulked, sometimes I would not talk, and when I refused, Nodier, as it was his own house, was compelled to talk; then everybody listened, small children and grown men and women. It was a combination of Walter Scott and Perrault, it was the scholar at daggers drawn with the poet, memory contending with imagination. Not only was Nodier entertaining to listen to, he was delightful to look at, as well. His long slender body, his long thin arms, his long white hands, his long face, overflowing with melancholy benevolence, — all were in harmony with his slightly drawling speech, in which there was at certain times a

marked Franche-Comtois accent which Nodier never
entirely lost. Ah! then the stream of talk was inexhaustible, always new, never the same thing twice over.
Time, space, history, nature were to Nodier the For-
tunatus' purse into which Pierre Schlemill plunged
his hands again and again and never found them empty.
He had known everybody: Danton, Charlotte Corday,
Gustavus III., Cagliostro, Pius VI., Catherine II.,
Frederic the Great, and the rest. Like the Comte de
Saint-Germain and the taratantaleo, he had been present
at the creation of the world and come down through the
centuries, changing his form. Indeed he had a most
ingenious theory on the subject of that change of form.
According to Nodier, dreams were simply a reminiscence
of days passed in another planet, of something that
happened long ago. According to Nodier, the most
fantastic dreams corresponded to actual occurrences in
bygone ages in Saturn, Venus, or Mercury; the strangest
images were simply the phantoms of figures that had
made a lasting impression upon our immortal souls.
When he first visited the museum of fossils at the
Jardin des Plantes, he cried out at the sight of animals
he had seen in the deluge of Deucalion and Pyrrha, and
sometimes he went so far as to admit that, observing the
tendency of the Templars to universal empire, he had
advised Jacques Molay to conquer his ambition. It
was not his fault that Jesus Christ was crucified; he
alone among his followers had warned him of Pilate's
evil designs upon him. Nodier had been especially
favored in meeting the Wandering Jew: the first time
at Rome, in the days of Gregory VII.; the second time
in Paris on the eve of St. Bartholomew, and the last
time at Vienne in Dauphiné; and he had some most
precious documents concerning him. And on that sub-

ject he corrected an error into which scholars and poets had fallen, especially Edgar Quinet. The name of the man with five sons was not Ahasuerus, which is half Greek and half Latin, but Isaac Laquedem. He could speak with assurance on that point, as he had the information from his own mouth. Then, from politics, from philosophy, from tradition, he would pass to natural history. Ah! how far Nodier outstripped in that science Herodotus, Pliny, Marco Polo, Buffon, and Lacépède! He had known spiders beside which Pélisson's spider was nothing. He had been intimate with frogs, compared with which Methuselah was only a child. Lastly, he had had business with caymans beside which the *tarasque* was only a lizard.

And then, too, such things happened to Nodier as happen only to men of genius. One day, when he was hunting for lepidoptera, during his sojourn in Styria, a land of granite cliffs and trees hoary with age, he climbed a tree in order to reach a cavity that he noticed, thrust his hand into the cavity, — as he was in the habit of doing, and most imprudently too, for one day he withdrew his arm from such a cavity decorated with a serpent that had coiled around it, — one day, as we were saying, having found a cavity, he thrust in his hand and felt something flabby and sticky, which yielded to the pressure of his fingers. He quickly drew his hand back and looked in: a pair of eyes gleamed with a dull flame in the cavity. Nodier believed in the devil; and so, when he saw those two eyes which were not unlike Charon's blazing eyes, as described by Dante, Nodier's first impulse was to fly. Then he reflected, thought better of it, took a hatchet, and, after measuring the depth of the hole, began to make an opening at the point where he supposed the unknown

object would be found.   At the fifth or sixth blow of
the hatchet the blood flowed from the tree precisely as
the blood flowed from Tasso's enchanted forest under
the sword of Tancred.   But it was not a lovely Amazon
that met his gaze, but a huge toad stuck fast in the
tree, into which he had probably been carried by the
wind when he was about the size of a bee.   How long
had he been there?   Two hundred, three hundred, five
hundred years perhaps.   He was five inches long and
three inches wide.

Another time — it was in Normandie, when he and
Taylor were making the tour of France — he went into
a church.   From one of the arches hung an enormous
spider and an enormous toad.   He applied to a peasant
for information concerning the strange couple.

And this is what the old peasant told him, after leading him to one of the flagstones in the floor of the
church, whereon was carved a recumbent knight in his
armor.

The knight was a baron of the olden time who had
left such an unsavory memory in the country that the
boldest men turned aside in order not to step on his
tomb, not from respect but from fear.   Above the tomb,
in fulfilment of a vow made by the knight on his death-
bed, a lamp was to burn night and day, the dead man
having left for the purpose a sum of money which was
much more than sufficient therefor.

One fine day, or rather one fine night, when, as it
happened, the curé was unable to sleep, looking from
his chamber window, which looked on the church, he
saw the lamp flicker and go out.   He attributed the
matter to an accident, and thought no more about it
that night.

But the next night, as he happened to wake about

two o'clock, it occurred to him to see if the lamp was burning. He got out of bed, went to the window, and saw *with his eyes* that the church was plunged in the most profound darkness.

That peculiar circumstance, occurring twice in forty-eight hours, assumed a certain seriousness. The next morning at daybreak, the curé sent for the beadle and accused him flatly of having put the oil in his salad instead of in the lamp. The beadle swore by all the gods that it was not so; that he had conscientiously filled the lamp every evening during the fifteen years he had held his office, and that it must be a trick of the wicked knight, who, after tormenting the living while he lived, was beginning to torment them again three hundred years after his death.

The curé declared that he placed implicit confidence in the beadle's word, but that he desired nevertheless to be present when the lamp was filled that evening. Consequently, at nightfall, the oil was poured into the receptacle and the lamp lighted in the curé's presence. When the lamp was lighted the curé locked the door of the church with his own hand, put the key in his pocket, and went home.

He took a breviary, made himself comfortable in a capacious arm-chair by the window, and waited, glancing alternately at the book and the church.

About midnight he saw the light which shone through the windows grow dim and die out.

That time it was certain that the occurrence was due to some strange, mysterious, inexplicable cause, in which the poor beadle could have had no part.

For a moment the curé thought that thieves had broken into the church, and were stealing the oil. But assuming that the offence was committed by thieves, they must be very honest rascals to confine themselves to stealing the oil and to leave the consecrated vessels unmolested.

It was not the work of thieves therefore. It must be due to some cause other than any that could be imagined, — a supernatural cause perhaps. The curé determined to discover the cause, whatever it might be.

The next evening he himself poured the oil into the lamp to make sure that he was not the victim of any trick of legerdemain. Then, instead of going out as he had done the night before, he hid in a confessional.

The hours passed, the lamp shone with a calm, undisturbed light. The clock struck twelve.

The curé thought that he heard a slight noise, as if a stone were moved from its place. Then he saw the shadow of an animal with gigantic paws, which shadow climbed a pillar, ran along the cornice, appeared for an instant against the arched roof, then slid down the cord and took up its position on the lamp, which began to grow dim, flickered, and went out.

The curé found himself in the most absolute darkness. He realized that he must repeat the experiment and take up a position nearer the scene of action.

Nothing could be easier. Instead of hiding in the confessional which was on the opposite side of the church from the lamp, he had only to hide in the one that was only a few steps away.

He did everything the next night as before, therefore, except that he changed to the other confessional and provided himself with a dark lantern.

Up to midnight there was the same tranquillity and silence, and the lamp performed its duty as honestly as ever. But at the last stroke of midnight there was the same creaking sound. But as it came from a spot within four steps of the confessional, the curé was able to fix his eyes at once upon that spot. The noise proceeded from the knight's tomb.

The carved flagstone which covered the sepulchre slowly rose, and through the aperture the curé saw a spider as large as a spaniel come forth, with hair six inches and claws an ell long; and the creature began at once, without hesitation, without looking about for a road which was evidently familiar to him, to climb the pillar, run along the cornice, slide down the cord, and finally drink the oil in the lamp, which went out as usual.

But the curé then had recourse to his dark lantern, and directed its rays upon the knight's tomb.

He thereupon perceived that the stone was held up by a toad as large as a porpoise, which raised it by inflating its body, and thus gave egress to the spider, which incontinently pumped out the oil, and then returned to divide with his companion.

Both had been living thus for centuries in that tomb, where they would in all probability be living to this day, had not an accident revealed to the curé the presence of a thief of some sort in his church.

The next day the curé summoned assistance. They raised the stone and put to death the insect and the reptile, whose bodies were suspended from the ceiling and bore witness to the extraordinary event.

Furthermore, the peasant who told Nodier the story was one of those who were called upon by the curé to fight those two fellow-occupants of the old knight's tomb, and as he had devoted his attention especially to the toad, a drop of the filthy creature's blood had dropped on his eye and had very nearly made him as blind as Tobias.

He had escaped with the loss of but one eye.

So far as Nodier was concerned, the stories of toads did not stop there.   There was in the longevity of those creatures something that charmed Nodier's imagination. And so all the tales of toads a hundred or a thousand years old he had at his tongue's end.   All the toads discovered in rocks or in tree-trunks, — from the one found in 1756 by the sculptor Leprince, at Eretteville, in a rock in which he was encased, to the one shut up in a plaster box by Hérifsant in 1771, and found very much alive in 1774 when the box was opened, were well known to him.   When any one asked Nodier what the wretched prisoners lived on, he would reply that they swallowed their skins.   He had made a close study of a fop of a toad who had a new skin six times in one winter, and swallowed the old one every time.   As for those found in the rocks that have existed since the beginning of the world, as, for instance, the one found in the quarry of Bourswick in Gothland, the state of absolute inaction in which they had necessarily lived, the suspension of life in a temperature which made dissolution impossible, and which did not require any loss of tissue to be made up, the moisture which kept alive the moisture in the animal's body and prevented its destruction by desiccation, — those things seemed to Nodier sufficient to justify a conviction in which there was as much faith as science.

Moreover Nodier had, as we have said, a certain natural humility, a certain tendency to belittle himself, which drew him toward the small and the humble. Nodier the bibliophile discovered unknown treasures in the way of books, which he rescued from the tomb of libraries.   So Nodier the philanthropist found among the living, unknown poets, whom he brought to light and led to celebrity. Injustice of every sort, oppression of every sort was revolting to him, and in his view mankind oppressed the toad, was unjust to him, and did not know or did not choose to know the toad's virtues. The toad was a faithful friend. Nodier had proved that fact by the story of the partnership of the toad and the spider, and, if called upon to do so, he would prove it twice over by telling another anecdote of a toad and a lizard no less interesting than the first. The toad was therefore not only a good friend, but a good father and a good husband. By delivering his wife himself, the toad gave to husbands the first lessons in conjugal love. By protecting the eggs of his family with his hind paws, and by carrying them on his back, the toad gave to heads of families the first lesson in paternity. As for the slaver which the toad exudes, or even squirts sometimes when he is tormented, Nodier declared that it was the most harmless substance in the world, and he preferred it to the saliva of many critics of his acquaintance.

It was not that those critics were not received at his house like other people, and received courteously too, but they gradually ceased to come of their own accord. They did not feel at ease in the atmosphere of kindliness which was the natural atmosphere of the Arsenal, and through which raillery flashed harmlessly, like the glow-worm on a lovely night at Nice or Florence; that is to say, it cast a gleam and vanished.

Conversing thus, we would draw near the end of a delightful dinner, during which all kinds of accidents, except upsetting the salt and placing a loaf of bread upside down, were taken philosophically. Coffee was served at the table. Nodier was at heart a sybarite. He had a thorough appreciation of that sentiment of the consummate sensualist, which brooks no moving about, no change of place between the dessert and the beverage that crowns the dessert. During that moment of pure Asiatic enjoyment, Madame Nodier would leave her seat to go and light the salon. As I did not take coffee, I frequently accompanied her. My long body was of great use to her in lighting the chandelier without standing on a chair.

The salon was not lighted until then, for, before dinner and on ordinary days, we were always received in Madame Nodier's bedroom. The candles lighted up walls painted white, with Louis XV. mouldings, and furniture of a very modest description, consisting of a dozen arm-chairs and a couch covered with red cashmere, window-curtains of the same color, a bust of Hugo, a statue of Henri IV., a portrait of Nodier, and an Alpine landscape by Regnier.

The guests entered the salon five minutes after it was lighted, Nodier last, leaning on Dauzat's arm, or on Bixio's or Francis Wey's or mine, always puffing and complaining as if he could hardly breathe. Then he would stretch himself out in a great arm-chair on the right-hand side of the hearth, his legs stretched out in front of him and his arms hanging, or else he would stand in front of the mantelpiece with his calves to the fire and his back to the mirror. If he stretched himself out in the arm-chair there was no hope. Nodier, absorbed by the momentary beatitude that coffee affords, proposed to play the egotist and to follow in silence the dream of his imagination; but if he leaned against the mantel, that was another matter: that meant that he was going to talk. Thereupon everybody would hold his peace and listen to one of the fascinating stories of his youth which seemed like a novel of Longus or an idyl of Theocritus; or to some melancholy drama of the Revolution, of which a battlefield in La Vendée or Place de la Révolution was always the stage; or to some mysterious conspiracy of Cadoudal or Oudet, Staps or Lahorie. They who came in while he was talking would not speak, but salute with a wave of the hand, and sit down or lean against the wall. At last the story would come to an end, as everything must. We never applauded, any more than we would applaud the murmuring of a brook or the song of a bird; but when the murmuring had died away, when the song had ceased, we listened still. Thereupon Marie, without speaking, would go to the piano, and suddenly a brilliant volley of notes would rush through the air like the prelude to a display of fireworks. At that signal the card-players, relegated to the corners of the room, would take their places at the tables and begin to play.

For a long time Nodier would play nothing but *bataille*. It was his favorite game, and he claimed to be very strong at it. At last he made a concession to the age and played écarté.

After the prelude Marie would sing some of Hugo's words or Lamartine's or mine, set to music by herself; and suddenly, in the midst of those fascinating melodies, which were always too short, we would hear the refrain of a contra-dance. Every gentleman would select his partner and a ball would begin.

A charming ball, for which Marie furnished all the music, tossing a word, amid the rapid trills executed by her fingers on the keys, to those who approached her in every "lady's chain," every "right and left," every "chassé across." From that moment Nodier vanished, and was completely forgotten. For he was not one of those high-handed, imperious masters whose presence you can feel, and whose approach you divine. He was the host of the days of antiquity, who effaces himself to make room for his guest, and who is content to be courteous, weak, and almost feminine.

Nodier, after disappearing for a moment or two, soon disappeared altogether. He went to bed, or rather he was put to bed early. Madame Nodier was intrusted with that duty. In winter she left the salon first, and sometimes, when there were no hot coals in the kitchen, we would see a warming-pan pass the door and return, filled, to the bedroom. Nodier followed the warming-pan, and that was the last of him.

Ten minutes later Madame Nodier would return to the salon. Nodier was safely in bed, and fell asleep to his daughter's melodies and the stamping and laughter of the dancers.

One day we found Nodier even more humble than usual. He was embarrassed, shamefaced. We asked him anxiously what the matter was.

Nodier had been chosen an Academician.

He apologized very humbly to Hugo and me.

But it was no fault of his. The Academy had chosen him when he least expected it.

The fact was that Nodier, who knew as much as all the academicians together, had demolished the Academy Dictionary stone by stone. He used to say that the Immortal who was assigned to write the article *crab* showed him one day what he had written, and asked him what he thought of it.

The article was in these words: —

" *Crab*, a small red fish, which walks backward."

"There's only one mistake in your definition," Nodier replied. "The crab is n't a fish, it is n't red, and it does n't walk backward. The rest is perfect."

I forgot to say that in due time Marie Nodier married, became Madame Ménessier; but her marriage made absolutely no change in the life at the Arsenal. Jules was the friend of all of us. We had long been accustomed to see him come to the house. He lived there now instead of coming there. That was all the difference.

I am wrong; a great sacrifice had been consummated. Nodier sold his library. Nodier loved his books, but he adored Marie.

I must say further that no one could make the reputation of a book as Nodier could. If he wished to sell a book or make a sale for it, he would write an article in praise of it. With what he discovered in it, he would make a unique copy. I remember the history of a volume entitled the " Zombi du Grand Pérou," which Nodier claimed was printed in the colonies, and the whole edition of which he destroyed on his own responsibility. The book was worth five francs, and he made it worth three hundred.

Four times Nodier sold his books, but he always kept a certain number, a precious nucleus, around which, in two or three years, his library would be reconstructed.

One day all our delightful meetings were interrupted. Nodier had been more ailing, more complaining for a month or two; but we had all become so accustomed to hear him complain that we paid no great attention to his complaints. With a disposition like Nodier's it is very hard to distinguish between real and imaginary suffering. This time, however, he was visibly growing weaker. No more sauntering along the quays, no more promenades on the boulevards, only a slow walk in the direction of Saint-Mandé when a last ray of the autumn sun forced its way through the gray clouds.

The end of the walk was a wretched wine-shop where

Nodier used to regale himself with brown bread in his
days of health.   He was, as a general rule, accompanied
by his whole family, except Jules, who was detained at
his office.   Madame Nodier, Marie, and the two children, Charles and Georgette, were not willing to leave
the husband, father, and grandfather.   They felt that
they had only a little time to be with him, and they
made the most of it.

Up to the last moment Nodier insisted that Sunday
should be observed as usual; but at last it was evident
that the sick man could no longer endure the noise and
movement in the salon.   One day Marie sadly informed
us that, on the following Sunday, the Arsenal would be
closed; but she added, in an undertone, to the most
intimate friends, —

"Come, and we will talk."

At last Nodier took to his bed, never to leave it again.
I went to see him.

"Ah! my dear Dumas," he said, holding out his
arms to me the moment he caught sight of me, "in the
days when I was in good health, you had only a friend
in me.   Since I have been sick, you have in me a
grateful debtor.   I cannot work any more, but I can
still read, and I am reading you, as you see; and when
I am tired I call my daughter and she reads you."

As he spoke he pointed to some of my books scattered
over his bed and the table.

It was a moment of genuine pride.   Nodier, isolated
from the world and unable to work, Nodier, that bound-
less mind, who knew everything, read me and found
entertainment in reading me!

I took his hands.   I would have liked to kiss them,
I was so grateful.

As it happened, I had read something of his the night

before, a small volume which had appeared in two numbers of the " Revue des Deux Mondes." It was " Inès de la Sierra."

I was lost in admiration. That novel, one of Charles' last works, was so fresh, so highly colored, that one would have said that it was a work written in his younger days, which he had found and sent into the world on the other slope of his life.

The story of Inès was a story of ghosts and phantoms and spectres; but, though it was entirely fanciful in the first part, it ceased to be so in the second. The end explained the beginning. Oh! I complained bitterly to Nodier of that explanation.

" True," he said, " I was wrong; but I have another. I won't spoil this one, never fear."

" I am glad to hear it, and when are you going to work on it?"

Nodier took my hand.

" This one I shall not spoil," he said, " because I shall not write it."

" Who will write it?"

" You."

" I, my dear Charles? Why, I don't know it.

" I will tell it to you. I have been keeping it for myself, or rather for you."

" My dear Charles, you shall tell it to me, but you must write it and print it yourself."

Nodier shook his head.

" I am going to tell it to you," he said. " If I recover, you can give it back to me."

" Wait till my next visit; we have time enough."

" My friend, I will say to you what I once said to a creditor when I gave him something on account: ' Take it when you can get it.' "

And he began.

Never did Nodier tell a story so entertainingly.

Oh! if I had had pen and paper, if I could have written as rapidly as he talked!

It was a long story, and I remained to dinner.

After dinner Nodier dozed. I left the Arsenal without seeing him again. That was the last time I ever saw him alive.

Nodier, whom everybody believed to be so ready to complain of trifles, had on the contrary concealed his suffering from his family until the very last. When he disclosed the wound, it was seen to be mortal.

Nodier was not only a Christian, but a stanch and true Catholic. He had made Marie promise to send a priest to him when the time arrived. The time arrived and Marie sent for the curé of Saint-Paul's.

Nodier confessed. Poor Nodier! There may have been many sins in his life, but there certainly was not one fault.

When the confession was finished the whole family entered the room.

Nodier was in a dark alcove, from which he held out his arms over his wife and daughter and grandchildren.

Behind the family were the servants.

Behind the servants the library; that is to say, those friends who never change, — books.

The curé read the prayers aloud, and Nodier made the responses aloud, like one familiar with the Christian liturgy. Then, when the prayers were at an end, he kissed them all, talked to them reassuringly about his condition, and said that he felt that he should live a day or two longer, especially if he was allowed to sleep for a few hours.

They left him alone, and he slept five hours.

On the evening of January 26th, the eve of his death, the fever increased, and caused some slight delirium. About midnight he could not recognize anybody, and his lips uttered incoherent words, among which could be distinguished the names of Tacitus and Fénélon.

About two o'clock death began to knock at the door. Nodier had a violent convulsion, and his daughter leaned over his pillow and held to his lips a cup filled with a quieting draught. He opened his eyes, looked at Marie, and recognized her by her tears. Then he took the cup from her hands and eagerly drank the liquid it contained.

"Did it taste good?" Marie asked him.

"Oh, yes! my child, like everything that comes from you."

Poor Marie let her head fall on the pillow, covering the dying man's moist forehead with her hair.

"Oh! if you would stay so," muttered Nodier, "I should never die." [1]

Death was still knocking.

The extremities began to grow cold; but as life was driven upward more and more, it concentrated in Nodier's brain, and made his mind clearer than it had ever been.

He blessed his wife and children, and then asked what day of the month it was.

"The 27th of January," said Madame Nodier.

"You won't forget that date, will you, my dears?" said he.

Then he turned to the window.

[1] Francis Wey has published a most interesting account of Nodier's last moments; but it was written for the intimate friends alone, and but twenty-five copies were printed.

" I would like to see the daylight once more," he said with a sigh.

He fell into a doze.

Then his breath became intermittent.

At last, just as the first ray of light shone in at the window, he opened his eyes, looked an adieu, and expired.

With Nodier everything died at the Arsenal, — joy, life, and light. We were all afflicted alike. Each one lost a part of himself in losing Nodier. For my own part, I do not just know how to express it, but there has been something dead within me since Nodier died.

That something lives only when I speak of Nodier.

That is why I speak of him so often.

The story you are about to read is the story Nodier told to me.

II.

THE HOFFMANN FAMILY.

AMONG the enchanting cities that are scattered along the banks of the Rhine like the beads of a rosary of which the river is the thread, we must include Mannheim, the second capital of the grand duchy of Baden and the second residence of the grand duke.

To-day, when the steamers which ascend and descend the Rhine stop at Mannheim, when a railroad runs to Mannheim, when Mannheim, with disheveled hair and blood-stained robe, has hoisted the standard of rebellion against her grand duke, amid the roar of musketry, I know not what Mannheim is; but I will tell you what it was at the period when this story begins, about fifty-six years ago.

It was the German city *par excellence*, at once tranquil and torn by political strife, a little melancholy, or rather a little dreamy; it was the city of Auguste Lafontaine's novels and of the poems of Gœthe, Henrietta Belmann, and Werther.

Indeed one needed but to cast a glance at Mannheim to make up one's mind at once, at sight of its squarely aligned houses, its division into four quarters, its fine, broad streets in which the grass grew, the shady promenade, between a double row of acacias, which runs through the city from end to end, to make up one's mind, I say, how smooth-flowing and tranquil life would be in such a paradise, were it not that sentimental or political passions sometimes placed a pistol in the hand of Werther or a dagger in the hand of Karl Ludwig Sand.

There is one square which has an entirely unique aspect: it is that on which the church and the theatre stand side by side.

Church and theatre were built at the same time, probably by the same architect; probably, too, about the middle of the last century, when the whims of a favorite had so great an influence upon art that one whole branch of art took her name, from the church to the little house of the kept mistress, from the bronze statue ten cubits high to the little figure in Saxony porcelain.

The church and theatre of Mannheim are in the Pompadour style.

The church has two exterior recesses: in one of them is a Minerva, in the other a Hebe.

The door of the theatre is surmounted by two sphinxes, representing Comedy and Tragedy.

One of the two sphinxes has a mask under his paw, the other a dagger. Both have their hair combed straight, with powdered *chignon*, which adds wonderfully to their Egyptian character.

The whole square, crooked houses, trimmed trees, festooned walls, have the same general character and form a most attractive whole.

A room on the first floor of a house whose windows look diagonally toward the doorway of the Jesuit church is the place to which we propose to conduct our readers, simply reminding them that we are taking them back more than half a century, and that the time is the year of grace, or disgrace, 1793, and the day, Sunday, the 10th of May. Everything is in bloom: the algæ on the bank of the river, the marguerites in the fields, the hawthorn in the hedges, the roses in the gardens, love in the heart.

Now let us add this: that one of the hearts which

were beating most violently in the whole city of Mannheim and its neighborhood was that of the young man
who occupied the little room we have mentioned, whose
windows looked diagonally toward the doorway of the
Jesuit church.

Room and young man both deserve a particular description.

The room was most assuredly the habitation of a mind
that was both whimsical and picturesque, for it had the
appearance of a studio, a music shop, and a study.

There were a palette, brushes, and an easel, and on the
easel an unfinished sketch.

There were a guitar, a viola, and a piano, and on the
piano an open sonata.

There were pen, ink, and paper, and on the paper was
scrawled the beginning of a ballad.

And along the walls there were bows and arrows,
slings of the fifteenth century, engravings of the six-
teenth, musical instruments of the seventeenth, chests of
all epochs, drinking vessels of all shapes, jugs of all
kinds, with glass necklaces, feather fans, stuffed snakes,
dried flowers, a whole world in fact; but a world not
worth twenty-five thalers in hard cash.

Was the occupant of the room a painter, a musician, or
a poet? We do not know.

But he certainly was a smoker; for among all his col-
lections, the most complete, the most prominent, occupy-
ing the place of honor and spread out in the sunlight
above an old couch, was a collection of pipes.

But whatever he may have been, poet, musician,
painter, or smoker, for the moment he was neither smoking, painting, writing scores, nor writing poetry.

No, he was looking.

He was standing like a statue against the wall, holding

his breath and looking; he was looking through his open window, having made a rampart of the curtain, in order to see without being seen; he was looking as one looks when the eyes are only the spectacles of the heart.

What was he looking at?

A spot entirely deserted at the moment, the doorway of the Jesuit church.

To be sure the doorway was deserted simply because the church was full.

Now let us say a word as to the personal appearance of the young man who occupied that room, who was looking out from behind the curtain, and whose heart beat so as he looked.

He was a young man of eighteen years at most, short and thin and wild of aspect. His long black hair fell from his forehead to below his eyes, which it veiled when he did not push it aside with his hand, and through the veil thus formed by his hair his eyes gleamed wildly, like the eyes of a man whose mental faculties are not likely always to remain in a state of perfect equilibrium.

This young man was neither poet, painter, nor musician; he was a compound of all three. He was painting, music, and poetry united; he was an eccentric, curious whole, good and bad, brave and timid, active and indolent. The young man, in a word, was Ernst Theodor Wilhelm Hoffmann.

He was born on a rough night in the winter of 1776, while the wind was blowing, the snow falling, and everybody who was not rich suffering. He was born at Königsberg, in the heart of Old Prussia; born so feeble and frail and puny, that his diminutive stature led every one to believe that it was much more important to order a grave dug for him than to buy a cradle. He was born in the same year in which Schiller, writing his drama of the

"Brigands," signed himself SCHILLER, the *slave of Klop-
stock;* born of one of the old middle-class families, such
as we had in France in the days of the Fronde, such as
there still are in Germany, but such as will soon cease to
exist anywhere in the world; born of a mother who was
of a sickly constitution, but devoutly resigned to her lot,
to which fact his whole unhealthy person owed its aspect
of attractive melancholy; born of a father of stern mind
and bearing, who was criminal councillor and commissioner of justice in the superior provincial tribunal. Beside the father and mother there were uncles who were
judges, bailiffs, burgomasters, and aunts still young and
fair and coquettish; and all, aunts and uncles alike, musicians, artists, full of energy and sprightliness. Hoffmann said that he had seen them. He remembered them
when he was a child of six and eight and ten years, giving
strange concerts, in which each one played on one of the
old instruments of which no one knows even the names
to-day: tympana, rebecs, zithers, citherns, *violes d'amour,*
and *violes de gamba.* To be sure, no one except Hoffmann had ever seen these musical uncles and aunts, all
of whom withdrew, one after another, like spectres, ex-
tinguishing, as they withdrew, the lights that burned in
their music-stands.

But of all those uncles there remained one; of all those
aunts there remained one.

That aunt was one of Hoffmann's most delightful
memories.

In the house in which Hoffmann had passed his youth,
there lived a sister of his mother, a young woman whose
sweet glances went to the very bottom of the soul; a
gentle, intellectual young woman, of remarkably keen
insight, who discerned in the child whom every one took
for a fool, a lunatic, or a maniac, signs of a powerful

mind; who alone pleaded for him,—with his mother, be
it understood; who predicted for him genius and renown,
a prediction that more than once brought tears to the eyes
of Hoffmann's mother, for she knew that disaster is the
inseparable companion of genius and renown.

That aunt was Aunt Sophia. She was a musician like
the whole family, and played the lute. When Hoffmann
awoke in his cradle, he awoke amid billows of delicious
melody; when he opened his eyes, he saw the young
woman's graceful form wedded to her instrument. She
was generally clad in a sea-green dress with red ribbons;
she was generally accompanied by an old musician with
crooked legs and a white wig, who played a bass-viol
taller than himself, to which he clung, running up and
down like a lizard on a gourd. From that torrent of
harmony, falling like a cascade of pearls from the fair
Euterpe's fingers, Hoffmann had imbibed the enchanted
potion that had made him a musician himself.

So it happened that Aunt Sophia was, as we have said,
one of Hoffmann's most delightful memories.

It was not so with his uncle.

The death of Hoffmann's father and his mother's ill-
health had left him in that uncle's hands.

He was a man as methodical as Hoffmann was unmethodical, as severely commonplace as Hoffmann was
strange and eccentric, and his passion for order and regularity was constantly exerted over his nephew, but always
as fruitlessly as the Emperor Charles the Fifth's will was
exerted over his clocks; the uncle labored in vain, the
clock struck according to his nephew's whim and not
according to his own.

In reality, despite his methodical habits and his regularity, this uncle of Hoffmann's was no bitter enemy of
art and the imagination. He would even tolerate music,

poetry, and painting; but he declared that no man of common sense would ever resort to such enervating pursuits, except to facilitate digestion, immediately after dinner. He arranged Hoffmann's life on this theory: so many hours for sleep, so many hours for his legal studies, so many hours for meals; so many minutes for painting, so many minutes for music, so many minutes for poetry.

Hoffmann would have liked to reverse the programme and say: so many minutes for study for the bar, and so many hours for poetry, painting, and music; but Hoffmann was not his own master. The result was that he had conceived a horror of the bar and of his uncle, and that one fine day he ran away from Kónigsberg with a few thalers in his pocket, and found his way to Heidelberg, where he halted for a few moments, but where he could not make up his mind to remain because of the wretched music at the theatre.

So he had gone from Heidelberg to Mannheim, whose theatre — near which he had, as we have seen, taken up his quarters — was reputed to rival France and Italy in lyric productions. We say France and Italy, because it must not be forgotten that it was only five or six years prior to the time of which we are writing that the great struggle took place between Gluck and Piccini.

Hoffmann, therefore, was at Mannheim, where he had lodgings near the theatre, and where he was living on the proceeds of his painting, his music, and his poetry, added to a few gold fredericks which his good mother sent him from time to time, at the moment when, assuming the privilege of the Lame Devil, we raise the ceiling of his room and exhibit him to our readers, standing like a statue against the wall behind his curtain, breathing hard, with his eyes fixed on the doorway of the Jesuit church.

III.

A LOVER AND A MADMAN.

JUST at the moment when a few persons who came out of the Jesuit Church, although the mass was hardly half finished, made Hoffmann more watchful than ever, some one knocked at his door. The young man shook his head, and stamped his foot impatiently, but did not reply.

The knock was repeated.

Hoffmann darted a fierce glance at the intruder through the door.

Again the knocking was repeated.

That time the young man stood absolutely motionless. He had evidently determined not to open the door.

But instead of persisting in knocking, the visitor contented himself by calling one of Hoffman's Christian names.

"Theodor," he said.

"Ah! it is you, Zacharias Werner," murmured the young man.

"Yes, it is I. Do you wish to be alone?"

"No, wait." And Hoffmann went and opened the door.

A tall young man, pale and thin and fair, and somewhat wild of aspect, entered the room. He was perhaps three or four years older than Hoffmann. As soon as the door opened, he put his hand on Hoffmann's shoulder and his lips to his forehead as an elder brother might have done.

He was, in fact, a true brother to Hoffmann. Born in the same house that he was, Zacharias Werner, the future author of " Martin Luther," " Attila," " The 24th of February," and the " Cross of the Baltic," had grown to manhood under the twofold protection of his own mother and Hoffmann's.

The two women, both of whom were subject to a nervous affection which ended in madness, had transmitted that malady to their children. Being weakened by the transmission, it became in Hoffmann's case capriciousness of the imagination, and in Werner's a melancholy temperament. The mother of the latter believed that, like the Blessed Virgin, she had a divine mission. Her child, her Zacharias, was to be the new Christ, the future Siloe promised by the Scriptures. While he slept she wove wreaths of bluebells which she placed on his brow. She knelt beside him, singing, in her sweet melodious voice, Luther's noblest chants, hoping, at every verse, to see the wreath of bluebells change to a halo.

The two children were brought up together. The fact that Zacharias was at Heidelberg, where he was studying, was Hoffmann's principal reason for flying from his uncle's, and Zacharias, repaying one good turn by another, had left Heidelberg and joined Hoffmann at Mannheim, when he went thither in quest of better music than he found at Heidelberg.

But when they were together at Mannheim, far removed from the influence of that sweet-natured mother, the young men were seized with an eager longing for travel, that indispensable complement to the education of the German student, and had determined to visit Paris. Werner, because of the strange spectacle that the capital of France must present in the throes of the Reign of Terror, which was at its height; Hoffmann, in order to compare French and Italian music, and especially to study the resources of the French opera in the matter of stage setting and scenery, for he had at that time the idea that he cherished throughout his life of becoming manager of a theatre.

Werner, a libertine by temperament, although religious by education, proposed at the same time to take advantage for his own pleasure of the strange freedom in the matter of morals at which the French people had arrived in 1793, and which one of his friends, recently returned from Paris, had described to him in such seductive colors, that the pleasure-loving student's head had been turned thereby.

Hoffmann intended to see the museums of which he had heard so many marvellous tales, and, being still uncertain as to his own style, to compare Italian painting with German painting.

Whatever the secret motives may have been that impelled the friends to visit France, the longing was equal in both cases.

To gratify that longing they lacked but one thing, — money. But, by a strange coincidence, chance decreed that Zacharias and Hoffmann had each received five gold fredericks from his mother on the same day.

Ten gold fredericks were equal to almost two hundred francs, and that was a very pretty little sum for two students, who spent but five thalers a month for board, lodging, and fuel. But that sum was entirely insufficient for the needs of the famous journey they had planned.

An idea had occurred to the two young men, and, as it had occurred to them both at once, they had taken it as an inspiration from heaven.

It was to go to a gambling-house and risk each his five gold fredericks.

With no more than the ten fredericks the journey was impossible. By risking them they might win enough to make the tour of the world.

It was no sooner said than done. The season for taking the waters was drawing near, and the gambling-houses had been open since the first of May. Werner and Hoffmann betook themselves to one of them.

Werner tried his luck first and lost his five fredericks in five minutes. It was Hoffmann's turn.

Hoffmann tremblingly risked his first gold frederick and won.

Encouraged by that beginning he doubled his stake. He had struck a vein of good luck. He won four times out of five, and he was one of those who have confidence in luck. Instead of hesitating he went boldly on, doubling and doubling. It was as if some supernatural power were assisting him. Without definite plan, without any sort of calculation, he staked his gold upon a card, and his gold doubled, trebled, quadrupled. Zacharias, trembling more violently than a fever patient, and paler than a ghost, murmured, " Enough, Theodor, enough; " but the gambler laughed at his childish timidity. Gold followed gold and gold begat gold. At last the clock struck two in the morning, the hour for closing had arrived, and the game ceased. The two young men loaded themselves down with gold, without stopping to count it. Zacharias, who could not believe that that wealth was all his, went out first. Hoffmann was about to follow him, when an old officer, who had not taken his eyes off him all the time he had been playing, stopped him as he was going out of the door.

" Young man," he said, laying his hand on Hoffmann's and gazing earnestly at him, " if you go on at this rate you will break the bank, I agree; but when the bank is broken, you will be only the surer prey for the devil."

He disappeared without waiting for Hoffmann to reply. Hoffmann also went out, but he was no longer the same man. The old soldier's prophecy had chilled him like an ice-cold bath, and the gold with which his pockets were filled weighed heavily upon him. It seemed to him as if he were carrying his burden of evil deeds.

Werner was waiting for him in high glee. They returned together to Hoffmann's lodging, one laughing and dancing and singing; the other lost in thought, almost dejected.

Both, however, decided to start for France the next day.

They embraced and parted.

Hoffmann, when he was alone, counted his gold.

He had five thousand thalers, twenty-three or twenty-four thousand francs.

He reflected a long while, and at last seemed to make up his mind to a difficult step.

While he was reflecting, by the light of a copper lamp, his face was pale and the perspiration was streaming from his brow.

At the slightest sound in the room, though it were as indistinguishable as the fluttering of a fly's wing, he started, turned his head and looked all around in alarm.

The officer's prediction returned to his mind. He murmured under his breath certain lines of " Faust," and he fancied that he could see on the threshold the gnawing rat, in the corner of his room the black spaniel.

At last his decision was made.

He put aside a thousand thalers which he considered amply sufficient for his journey, and tied the other four thousand thalers in a bundle. Then he fastened a card upon the bundle with wax, and wrote on the card, —

"To the Herr Burgomaster of Königsberg, to be distributed among the poorest families of the town."

Then, content with the victory he had won over himself, comforted by what he had done, he undressed, went to bed, and slept without waking until seven o'clock in the morning.

At seven o'clock he awoke, and his first glance was for his thousand visible thalers and the sealed package containing the other four thousand. He thought that he had been dreaming.

The sight of the gold assured him of the reality of what had happened the night before.

But the thing that was most real to Hoffmann, although there was no material object to remind him of it, was the old officer's prediction.

And so, without the slightest regret, he dressed as usual; and, taking his four thousand thalers under his arm, he carried them himself to the office of the Königsberg diligence, having first taken the precaution to deposit the thousand thalers in his drawer.

Then, as it had been agreed, as the reader will remember, that the two friends should start for France that evening, Hoffmann began to make his preparations for the journey.

As he went and came, now brushing a coat, now folding a shirt, now sorting out his handkerchiefs, Hoffmann cast his eyes into the street, and remained standing in the attitude he had assumed at that instant.

A young girl of sixteen or seventeen years, a fascinating creature, certainly a stranger in Mannheim, as Hoffmann did not know her by sight, was coming from the other end of the street toward the church.

Hoffmann had never seen her like in all his dreams as poet, painter, or musician.

She not only surpassed all that he had ever seen, but all that he hoped to see.

And yet he was so far away that he could see only a ravishing *ensemble*. The details eluded him.

The girl was attended by an old serving-woman. They slowly ascended the church steps together and disappeared under the doorway.

Hoffman left his trunk half packed, a wine-colored coat half brushed, his frogged coat half folded, and remained motionless behind his curtain.

That is where we found him, waiting for her whom he had seen go in to come out.

He dreaded but one thing, — that she was an angel, and that, instead of coming out by the door, she would fly out through the window on her way back to heaven.

It was in that situation that we caught him, and that his friend Zacharias caught him after us.

The new-comer, as we have said, placed his hand on his friend's shoulder, and his lips on his brow simultaneously.

Then he heaved a deep sigh.

Although Zacharias Werner was always pale, he was paler than usual at that moment.

"What's the matter?" Hoffmann asked with unfeigned anxiety.

"O my friend!" cried Werner. "I am a brigand! I am a villain! I deserve death! Cleave my head with an axe, pierce my heart with an arrow. I am no longer worthy to look upon the light of heaven."

"Nonsense!" said Hoffmann, with the placidly absent-minded air of the happy man, "what has happened to you, my dear friend?"

"What has happened? You asked me what has happened, didn't you? Well, my friend, the devil tempted me!"

"What do you mean?"

"That when I saw all my gold this morning, there was so much of it that it seemed to me as if I must have dreamed about it."

"Dreamed about it?"

"There was a table all covered with it," Werner continued. "Well, when I saw it, a veritable fortune, a thousand gold fredericks, my friend, — when I saw it all, when I saw every piece gleaming like the sun, a frenzy seized me. I could not resist. I took a third of my money and went to the gambling-house."

"And you lost?"

"To my last kreutzer."

"What's the odds? It's a small matter, as you have two-thirds left."

"Ah, yes! two-thirds! I went back and got the second third and —"

"And you lost it like the first?"

"More quickly, my friend, more quickly."

"And then you went back and got the last third?"

"I didn't go back, I flew. I took the fifteen hundred francs that were left and put them on the red."

"In that case," said Hoffmann, "black came up, I presume?"

"Ah! my friend, black, the horrible black, without hesitation, without remorse, as if it did not, by coming

up, snatch away my last hope! Gone, my friend,
gone!"

"And you regret the loss of the thousand fredericks
solely on account of our journey?"

"For no other reason. Oh! if I had only put aside
enough to take me to Paris — five hundred thalers!"

"Then you would be consoled for the loss of the
rest?"

"Instantly."

"Ah, well! set your mind at rest at once, my dear
Zacharias," said Hoffmann, leading him to his desk.
"There are your five hundred thalers, — go."

"What! you bid me go?" cried Werner. "What
about yourself?"

"Oh! I do not intend to go."

"You don't intend to go?"

"No, not at this moment, at all events."

"But why not? What is your reason? What pre-
vents your going? What keeps you at Mannheim?"

Hoffmann hastily drew his friend to the window.
The mass was at an end, and people were beginning to
leave the church.

"There, look, look!" he said, pointing out somebody
to Werner with his finger.

The unknown girl appeared at that moment in the
doorway and slowly descended the church steps, her
prayer-book against her breast, her eyes cast down, as
modest and pensive as Goethe's Gretchen.

"Do you see?" murmured Hoffmann. "Do you
see?"

"Certainly I see."

"Well, what do you say?"

"I say that there's no woman for whom it is worth
sacrificing a trip to Paris, though she were the fair

Antonia, daughter of old Gottlieb Murr, the new leader of the orchestra at the Mannheim theatre."

" You know her then ? "

" Certainly."

" And you know her father ? "

" He led the orchestra at the Frankfort theatre."

" Can you give me a letter to him ? "

" Surely."

" Sit you down there, Zacharias, and write."

Zacharias sat down at the table and wrote.

On the eve of his departure for France he commended his young friend Theodor Hoffmann to his old friend Gottlieb Murr.

Hoffmann hardly gave Zacharias time to finish his letter. As soon as he had signed his name, he took it, and, after embracing his friend, rushed from the room.

" Never mind," Zacharias Werner called after him. " You will see that the woman does n't live, however pretty she may be, who can make you forget Paris."

Hoffmann heard his friend's words, but did not think best to turn and respond to them even by a gesture of assent or dissent.

Zacharias Werner put his five hundred thalers in his pocket, and, in order to avoid any further temptation by the demon of play, ran as fast toward the stage-office as Hoffmann ran toward the house of the old leader of the orchestra.

Hoffmann knocked at Gottlieb Murr's door at the same moment that Werner entered the Strasburg diligence.

IV.

MASTER GOTTLIEB MURR.

THE leader of the orchestra in person opened the door
to Hoffmann.

Hoffmann had never seen Master Gottlieb, and yet
he recognized him. Grotesque as he was in appearance,
he could be nothing but an artist, and a great artist at
that.

He was a little old man of some fifty-five to sixty
years, with one crooked leg which resembled a corkscrew, and yet he did not limp overmuch. As he
walked, or rather hopped, — his hop greatly resembled a
wagtail's, — as he hopped along in front of the persons
he admitted to his house, he would suddenly stop,
make a pirouette on his crooked leg, as if he were
screwing a gimlet into the floor, and then go forward
again.

Hoffmann, as he followed him, examined him closely
and engraved upon his mind one of those marvellous,
weird portraits of which he has given us such a complete
gallery in his works.

The old man's face was enthusiastic, shrewd, and
intellectual at once, covered with parchment-like skin,
spotted red and black like a page of plain-song. In the
middle of that curious surface gleamed two bright eyes,
whose keen glance one could the better appreciate
because the spectacles that he wore and never laid aside,
even in his sleep, were invariably on top of his head or

at the end of his nose. It was only when he was playing on the violin, with head erect and looking off into
the distance, that he really used what seemed to be
rather a luxury than a necessity to him.

His head was bald and always protected by a black
cap, which had become an inherent part of his person.
Day and night Master Gottlieb received his visitors in
his cap. And when he went out he simply wore a
small Jean-Jacques wig over it; so that the cap was
confined between the wig and his skull. It goes without saying that Master Gottlieb never troubled himself
in the least about the bit of velvet that protruded from
under his false hair, which being more closely connected
with the hat than with the head, accompanied the hat
in its aerial excursions whenever Master Gottlieb saluted
an acquaintance.

Hoffmann looked about, but saw nobody.

So he followed Master Gottlieb, who, as we have
said, walked in front of him, wherever he chose to
lead.

Master Gottlieb paused in a large study filled with
scores piled one upon another, and loose sheets of
music. Upon a table were ten or twelve boxes, more
or less ornate, and all of the shape which no musician
ever mistakes, the shape of a violin case.

At that moment Master Gottlieb was engaged in
arranging Cimarosa's "Matrimonio Segreto" for the
Mannheim theatre, where he proposed to try some
Italian music as an experiment.

A bow was thrust in his belt, like Harlequin's club,
or, more properly speaking, was held in place by the
buttoned pocket of his breeches. A pen was perched
proudly behind his ear, and his fingers were smeared
with ink.

With his ink-smeared fingers he took the letter Hoffmann handed him, and said, as he glanced at the address and recognized the handwriting, —

"Ah! Zacharias Werner, a poet, yes, a poet, but a gambler." Then he added, as if the virtue atoned somewhat for the vice, "A gambler, a gambler, but a poet."

He unsealed the letter.

"Gone, has he not?" he said. "Gone!"

"He is starting at this moment."

"God guide his steps!" said Gottlieb, raising his eyes to heaven as if to commend his friend to God. "But he has done well to go. Travelling forms youth, and, if I had not travelled, I should not know the immortal Paesiello, the divine Cimarosa."

"But you would know their works just as well, Master Gottlieb," said Hoffmann.

"Yes, their works, of course; but what does it amount to, to know the work without knowing the artist? It is like knowing the soul without the body. The work is the ghost, the apparition. The work is what remains of us after our death. But the body, you see, is what has lived. You will never thoroughly comprehend a man's work unless you have known the man himself."

Hoffmann nodded his head.

"It is true," he said. "I never fully appreciated Mozart until I had seen him."

"Yes, yes," said Gottlieb. "Mozart has some good points; but why has he those good points? Because he travelled in Italy. German music, young man, is the music of men; but mark this, Italian music is the music of the gods."

"But it was not in Italy," suggested Hoffmann with a smile, "it was not in Italy that Mozart wrote the

'Marriage of Figaro' and 'Don Juan,' for he wrote one in Vienna for the emperor and the other at Prague for the Italian theatre there."

"True, young man, true, and I like to find in you the national spirit that leads you to stand up for Mozart. Yes, if the poor devil had lived and had taken one or two more journeys to Italy, he would certainly have been a master, a very great master. But, take this 'Don Juan' that you speak of, and this 'Marriage of Figaro,' — for what did he compose them? For Italian libretti, Italian words, with a reflection of the sunlight of Bologna, Rome, or Naples. Believe me, young man, one must have seen and felt that sunlight to appreciate it at its true worth. Look you, I left Italy four years ago. For four years I have shivered except when I have thought of Italy. The mere thought of it warms me. I need no cloak when I think of Italy. I need no coat, I need no cap even. The memory gives me new life. O music of Bologna! O sun of Naples! Oh!—"

For a moment the old man's face expressed supreme beatitude, and his whole body seemed to thrill with indescribable bliss, as if the hot waves of the southern sun were still pouring down upon his bald head, thence to his shoulders, and from his shoulders over his whole body.

Hoffmann was careful not to arouse him from his trance, but availed himself of the opportunity to look about, still hoping to see Antonia. But the doors were closed, and there was no sound behind any of them to indicate the presence of a living being.

He had no choice, therefore, but to return to Master Gottlieb, whose ecstasy gradually became less absorbing, until he finally emerged from it with a sort of shudder.

"Brrrr! you were saying, young man?" he said.

Hoffmann started.

"I was saying, Master Gottlieb, that, being a musician, I have come to you at the suggestion of my friend Zacharias Werner, who has told me of your kindness to young men."

"Oho! you are a musician!"

And Gottlieb drew himself up, raised his head, threw it back, and looked at Hoffmann through his spectacles, which at that moment were resting on the extreme end of his nose.

"Yes, yes," he muttered, "a musician's head, a musician's brow, a musician's eye. What are you? composer or performer?"

"Both, Master Gottlieb."

"Both!" exclaimed Master Gottlieb. "Both! these young people are n't afraid of anything! It requires the whole life of a man, yes, of two men, of three men, to be either, and they are both, forsooth!"

He threw up his arms and whirled around as if he would bore a hole in the floor with his corkscrew of a right leg.

Having completed his pirouette, he came to a standstill in front of Hoffmann.

"Well, presumptuous youth," he said, "what have you done in the way of composition?"

"Sonatas, sacred music, quintettes."

"Sonatas, after Sebastian Bach! sacred music, after Pergolese! quintettes, after Francis Joseph Haydn! Ah! youth! youth! And as a performer," he added with an accent of profound pity, "as an instrumentalist, what instrument do you play?"

"Almost all, from the rebeck to the harpsichord, from the *viole d'amour* to the theorbum: but the instrument to which I have paid most attention is the violin."

"Indeed," said Master Gottlieb satirically, "you have really done the violin that honor! Upon my word, it is a great piece of good fortune for the poor violin! Why, you wretched boy!" he added, hopping back to Hoffmann on a single leg to go the faster, "do you know what the violin is? The violin!" and Master Gottlieb balanced himself on the one leg we have mentioned, the other remaining in the air like a crane's; "the violin! why, it is the most difficult of all instruments. The violin was invented by Satan himself for the damnation of mankind, when he was at the end of his inventions. Satan has destroyed more souls with the violin than with the seven capital sins combined. Only the immortal Tartini — Tartini, my master, my hero, my god! — he was the only one who ever attained perfection on the violin. But he alone knows what it cost him in this world and the other to play a whole night with the devil's own violin and keep the bow. Oh! the violin! Do you know, sacrilegious youth, that that instrument conceals beneath its almost pitiful simplicity the most inexhaustible treasures of harmony that it is possible for man to drink from the cup of the gods? Have you studied the frame, the strings, the bow, the horsehair, the horsehair above all? Do you aspire to combine, to unite, to subdue under your fingers all the parts of that marvellous whole, which has resisted for two centuries the efforts of the greatest masters, which groans and laments and complains under their fingers, and has never sung except under the fingers of the immortal Tartini, my master? When you took up a violin for the first time, did you realize what you were doing, young man? But you are

not the first," added Master Gottlieb, with a sigh
drawn from the inmost recesses of his being, "and you
will not be the last to be undone by the violin. The
violin, everlasting tempter! Others besides yourself
have believed in their calling, and have wasted their
lives scraping the strings, and you are going to increase
the number of those poor wretches, who are already so
numerous, so useless to society, and so insufferable to
their fellow-creatures."

Suddenly, without any transition, he seized a violin
and a bow, as a fencing-master takes a pair of foils, and
handed them to Hoffmann.

"Come," he said, in a defiant tone, "play me something. Play, and I will tell you where you stand; and
if you still have time to draw back from the precipice,
I will rescue you as I rescued poor Zacharias Werner.
He also played the violin. He played it fiercely, with
frenzy. He dreamed of performing miracles, but I
opened his eyes. He broke his violin into small pieces
and burned them up. Then I put a bass-viol in his
hands, and that finished calming him down. There was
room on that for his long, thin fingers. At first he
made them do their ten leagues an hour, and now he
plays the bass-viol well enough to serenade his uncle on
his birthday, whereas he never would have played the
violin except to serenade the devil."

Hoffmann took the violin and looked it over.

"Yes, yes," said Master Gottlieb. "You look to
see who made it, as the gourmand smells of the wine
before drinking. Pick a string, just one, and if your
ear doesn't tell you the maker's name you are not
worthy to touch it."

Hoffmann picked a string, which gave forth a pro-
longed, shivering, vibrating note.

" It 's an Antonio Stradivarius. "

" Well, well, not bad; but of what period of Stradivarius' life? Let us see how far you can go. He made many violins between 1698 and 1728. "

" Oh! as to that," said Hoffmann, " I confess my ignorance, and it seems to me impossible — "

" Impossible, blasphemer! impossible! that 's as if you were to tell me that it 's impossible to tell the age of wine by tasting it. Listen to me: As truly as this is the 10th day of May, 1793, that violin was made during the journey of the immortal Antonio from Cremona to Mantua in 1705, when he left his workshop in charge of his first assistant. So that that Stradivarius, I am happy to tell you, is only a third-rate instrument; but I greatly fear that it is still too good for a poor schoolboy like you. Ha! ha! ha! "

Hoffmann put the violin to his shoulder, and, not without a violent pulsation of the heart, began to play variations on the theme from " Don Juan," —

" La ci darem' la mano."

Master Gottlieb stood beside him, beating time with his head and with the foot at the end of his crooked leg. As Hoffmann played on, his face lighted up, his eyes shone, his upper teeth gnawed his lower lip, and on either side of that same lip protruded a tooth, which under ordinary circumstances it was intended to conceal, but which stood out at that moment like a boar's tusks. Finally, an allegro movement, over which Hoffmann achieved a signal triumph, extorted from Master Gottlieb a nod resembling a sign of approbation.

Hoffmann ended with a flourish which he thought extremely brilliant, but which, far from satisfying the old musician, caused him to make a wry face.

His face gradually resumed its serenity, however, and he said, bringing his hand down on the young man's shoulder, —

"Well, well, it's not so bad as I supposed. When you have forgotten all you have learned, when you have ceased to indulge in those fashionable gymnastics, when you get the better of those jerky fits and those shrieking flourishes, something can be done with you."

Such praise, from a man so hard to please as the old musician, delighted Hoffmann beyond measure. Nor did he forget, swimming as he was in the musical ocean, that Gottlieb was the lovely Antonia's father.

So, taking on the bound the words the old man let fall, he asked, —

"Who will undertake to do something with me? Will you, Master Gottlieb?"

"Why not, young man? Why not, if you are willing to listen to old Murr?"

"I will listen to you, master, as long as you choose."

"Ah!" murmured the old man in a melancholy tone, for his glance wandered back into the past, and his memory was busy with bygone days, "I have known many virtuosi! I knew Corelli, — by tradition, it is true. He it was who opened the road, who hewed out the path. One must either play as Tartini played or give up playing. He was the first to divine that the violin is a god, or, at least, a temple from which a god may emerge. After him comes Paganini, a fair, intelligent violinist, but soft, too soft, especially in certain *appoggiamenti*. Then Germiniani, a powerful performer, but powerful by fits and starts, without transition. I went to Paris expressly to see him, as you propose to go to see the opera, — a maniac, my friend, a sleep-walker, my friend, a man who gesticulated in

his dreams, quick to hear the *tempo rubato*, fatal
tempo rubato, which kills more musicians than the
smallpox, the yellow fever, or the plague! Then I
played my sonatas to him in the style of my master, the
immortal Tartini, and he admitted his error. Unfortunately the pupil was buried up to the neck in his
method. He was seventy-one years old, poor child!
Forty years earlier I would have saved him, like
Giardini. Him I took in time, but unfortunately he
was incorrigible. The devil himself had taken possession of his left hand, and it would go and go and go at
such a rate that his right hand could not follow it.
Such fantasias and frills and flourishes! They were
enough to give a Dutchman Saint Vitus' dance. And
one day, when he was spoiling a magnificent passage in
Jomelli's presence, dear Jomelli, who was the best
fellow in the world, gave him such a smart rap that
Giardini's cheek was swollen for a month, and Jomelli
had his hand in bandages for three weeks. He was like
Lulli, a madman, a downright madman, a rope-dancer,
a performer of dangerous leaps, an equilibrist without a
balancing rod, who should be given a balancing rod
instead of a bow. Alas! alas! alas!" cried the old
man piteously. "With a feeling of profound despair
I say it, but with Nardini and me the noble art of
violin-playing will die out; the art by which our common master Orpheus attracted animals, moved rocks, and
built cities. Instead of building up, like the divine
violin, we demolish, like the accursed trumpets. If
the French ever enter Germany, if they want to beat
down the walls of Philippsburg, which they have
besieged so many times, they will only have to allow
four violinists of my acquaintance to give a concert
before the gates."

The old man paused to take breath, then resumed in a milder tone, —

"I know that there is Viotti, one of my own pupils, a boy with the best will in the world, but impatient, impudent, and unmethodical. As for Giarnowicki, he's an ignorant fool, and the first thing I told my old Lisbeth was to close my door in hot haste if she ever heard that name pronounced outside it. Thirty years Lisbeth has been with me, but I tell you, young man, I shall discharge Lisbeth if she ever lets Giarnowicki into my house, — a Sarmatian, a Welshman, who dared speak ill of the master of masters, the immortal Tartini! Oh! I'll give lessons and advice gratis as long as he wants to the man who brings me Giarnowicki's head. As for you, my boy," continued the old man, returning to Hoffmann, "as for you, you are not very strong yet, it is true; but Rode and Kreutzer, my pupils, were no stronger than you; and I was saying that by coming to see Master Gottlieb, in applying to Master Gottlieb, in procuring a recommendation to him from a man who knows and appreciates him, that madman, Zacharias Werner, you prove that there is an artist's heart in that breast. And so, young man, I do not now propose to put an Antonio Stradivarius in your hands; nor even a Gramulo, that old master whom the immortal Tartini esteemed so highly that he never played except upon Gramulos. No, but an Antonio Amati, the grandfather, the ancestor, the original parent stock of all the violins that have ever been made, — that instrument, which will be my Antonia's marriage portion, is the one upon which I wish now to hear you play. It is Ulysses' bow, you see, and whoever can bend Ulysses' bow is worthy of Penelope."

Thereupon the old man opened a velvet case lined

with rich gold lace, and took from it such a violin as,
it seemed, could never have existed before, and such as
Hoffmann alone perhaps could remember having seen in
the imaginary concerts given by his great-uncles and
great-aunts.

He bent over the venerable instrument and said, as
he handed it to Hoffmann, —

"Take it, and try not to be too unworthy of it."

Hoffmann bowed, took the instrument with respect,
and began an old *étude* by Sebastian Bach.

"Bach, Bach," muttered Gottlieb. "He is well
enough for the organ, but he knew nothing about the
violin. No matter."

At the first note Hoffmann drew from the instrument,
he started, for he was enough of a musician to realize
what a treasure-house of melody had been placed in his
hands.

The bow was so curved that it enabled the player to
touch all four strings at once, and the last string soared
aloft to celestial notes of such marvellous beauty as
Hoffmann had never dreamed could be produced by the
hand of man.

Meanwhile the old man stood near him, with his
head thrown back, blinking his eyes, and saying, by
way of encouragement, —

"Not bad, not bad, young man; the right hand, the
right hand! The left hand is only the movement; the
right hand is the soul. Come, soul! soul!! soul!!!"

Hoffmann felt that old Gottlieb was right, and he
realized the truth of what he told him at first, that he
would have to unlearn all that he had learned; and, by
an insensible but constant transition, he passed from
pianissimo to *fortissimo*, from caresses to threats, from
the lightning flash to the thunderbolt and lost himself

in a torrent of melody which rose like a cloud and fell in rippling cascades, in liquid pearls, in damp spray; and he was under the influence of a new mental condition, of a state bordering on ecstasy, when suddenly his left hand relaxed its hold on the strings, the bow stood still in his right hand, the violin slipped from his shoulder, his eyes became fixed upon a certain point and glowed like live coals.

The door had opened, and Hoffmann, looking in the mirror in front of which he was playing, saw the fair Antonia appear in the doorway like a phantom evoked by a divine melody, her mouth partly open, her breast heaving, her eyes moist.

Hoffmann uttered an exclamation of pleasure, and Master Gottlieb had barely time to save the venerable Antonio Amati as it dropped from the young violinist's hand.

V.

ANTONIA.

ANTONIA appeared a thousand times more beautiful to Hoffmann when she opened the door and crossed the threshold, than when he saw her descending the church steps.

It was because he was able to grasp at a single glance, in the mirror in which the young girl's image was reflected, and which was within two steps, all the points of beauty which had escaped him at a distance.

Antonia was barely seventeen years old. She was of medium height, rather tall than short, but so slender without being thin, so willowy without being weakly built, that all the timeworn comparisons to a lily swaying on its stalk, to a palm-tree bending in the wind, would have failed to do justice to the Italian *morbidezza*, the only word that expresses the idea of gentle languor which the sight of her aroused. Her mother was, like Juliet, one of the loveliest flowers of the springtime of Verona, and in Antonia were found, not blended, but side by side,—and it was in that that the girl's charm consisted,—the beauties of the two races which dispute for the palm of beauty. Thus, with the fine texture of skin, characteristic of the women of the North, she had the dead white color of the women of the South; thus her fine, thick flaxen hair, flying about in the slightest breeze like a golden vapor, shaded eyes and eyebrows of a velvety black. Strangely enough, the harmonious commingling of the two races was especially noticeable in her voice. So, when Antonia spoke German, the soft accents of the beautiful language in which, as Dante says, the *si* plays so prominent a part, softened the harshness of the Germanic accent, whereas, on the other hand, when she spoke Italian, the somewhat too flexible tongue of Metastasio and Goldoni assumed a firmness imparted to it by the virile strength of the tongue of Schiller and Goethe.

Nor was this fusion to be remarked on the physical side only. Antonia was mentally a marvellous and rare example of what the sun of Italy and the fogs of Germany can perform in the way of combining widely contrasted forms of poesy. You would have said that she was at once a muse and a fairy, the Beatrice of the " Divina Commedia " and the Lorelei of the ballad.

The fact was that Antonia, the artiste *par excellence*, was the daughter of a great artiste. Her mother, who had been brought up in the Italian school, fought a hand to hand fight one day with German music. The score of Gluck's " Alcestis " had fallen into her hands, and she induced her husband, Master Gottlieb, to translate the poem into Italian. When it was translated, she sang it at Vienna; but she presumed too much upon her strength, or rather, wonderful songstress that she was, she did not know the measure of her own sensitiveness. At the third performance of the opera, — which had achieved the greatest success, — in Alcestis' beautiful solo, —

" Divinities of Styx, ye ministers of death,
I 'll not invoke your cruel sympathy.
I rescue a fond husband from his mournful fate,
But I abandon to you a true, faithful wife," —

when she reached the *D*, which she gave with the full strength of her lungs, she turned pale, staggered and

fainted: a blood-vessel had burst in that swelling chest;
the sacrifice to the infernal gods was consummated in
reality; Antonia's mother was dead.

Poor Master Gottlieb was leading the orchestra. From
his desk he saw her whom he loved above all things turn
pale, stagger and fall; more than that, he heard the chord
break upon which her life depended, and he uttered a
terrible shriek which mingled with the last breath of the
dying artiste.

Therein, perhaps, lay the secret of Master Gottlieb's
hatred for the German masters. It was Gluck who, inno-
cently to be sure, had caused the death of his Teresa;
but he hated Gluck none the less with a deadly hatred,
because of the profound grief he had suffered, which had
not been allayed until he began to transfer to Antonia as
she grew to girlhood all the love he had had for her
mother.

At seventeen, the age at which she had now arrived,
the girl had taken the place of everything else in the old
man's life; he lived and breathed in Antonia. The
thought of her death had never presented itself to his
mind; but, even if it had so presented itself, he would
not have been seriously disturbed, because it would never
have occurred to him that he could survive Antonia.

And so the appearance of Antonia at the door of his
study was welcomed by him no less enthusiastically than
by Hoffmann, although the father's feeling was very different in kind.

The girl came forward slowly; her eyes were bright
with tears. She walked up to Hoffmann, put out her
hand, and said, with modest familiarity, as if she had
known the young man ten years,—

"Good morning, brother."

Master Gottlieb had remained silent and motionless

from the moment his daughter appeared. His heart, as was always the case, had left his body, and was fluttering about her, singing in her ears all the melodies of love and joy that a father's heart can sing at sight of his beloved daughter.

He had placed his cherished Antonio Amati on the table, and, clasping his hands as he would have done before the Virgin, he watched his child approach.

As to Hoffmann, he did not know whether he was asleep or awake, whether he was in heaven or on earth, whether it was a woman or an angel coming to him.

So it was that he almost recoiled when Antonia drew near and offered him her hand, calling him her brother.

"You, my sister!" he said, in a stifled voice.

"Yes," said Antonia. "It is not blood that makes the family, but the mind. All flowers are sisters by their perfume, all artists are brothers by their art. I have never seen you, it is true, but I know you; your bow has told me the story of your life. You are a poet, a little mad, my poor friend! Alas! it is the glowing spark that God confines in our heads or in our hearts that consumes our brains or our hearts."

Then she turned to Master Gottlieb.

"Good morning, father," she said, "why have you not kissed your Antonia? Ah! I understand: 'Il Matrimonio Segreto,' 'Stabat Mater,' Cimarosa, Pergolese, Porpora. What is Antonia beside those great geniuses? a poor child who loves you, but whom you forget for them."

"I forget you!" cried Gottlieb, "old Murr forget Antonia! The father forget his daughter! For what? for a parcel of wretched notes, for a collection of semibreves and quavers, of white notes and black notes, of flats and sharps! Oh, yes! see how I forget you!"

He whirled about on his crooked leg with astounding agility, and with his other leg and both hands sent flying about the room the different parts of the score of "Il Matrimonio Segreto," which were all ready to be distributed to the members of the orchestra.

"Father! father!" said Antonia.

"Fire! fire!" cried Master Gottlieb, "give me fire that I may burn them all: Pergolese, Cimarosa, Paesiello, my Stradivariuses, my Gramulos, and my Antonio Amati! Has not my child, my Antonia, said that I love chords, wood, and paper better than my own flesh and blood? Fire! fire!! fire!!!"

The old man ran about like a madman, hopped on his crooked leg like the Lame Devil, and waved his arms like a windmill.

Antonia watched the old man's frenzy with the sweet smile of satisfied filial pride. She knew well — she who had never played the flirt with any man but her father — that her power over the old man was without bounds, that his heart was a kingdom in which she reigned an absolute sovereign. So she stopped him in the midst of his evolutions, and, drawing him toward her, deposited a simple kiss on his forehead.

The old man uttered a cry of joy, took his daughter in his arms, lifted her up as if she were a bird, and after twisting around on his leg three or four times, sank at last upon a capacious couch, where he began to rock her as a mother rocks her child.

At first Hoffman had gazed at Master Gottlieb in dismay; when he saw him scatter the sheets of music about, he believed that he was a raving maniac. But he was speedily reassured by Antonia's tranquil smile, and he respectfully collected the scattered sheets and placed them on the tables and stands, glancing out of the corner of his

15

eye all the while at the strange group, in which even the old man made a poetic figure.

Suddenly something soft, sweet, ethereal passed through the air, a breath of vapor, a melody, yes, something even more divine: it was Antonia's voice attacking, in obedience to her artistic caprice, that wonderful composition of Stradella's which saved its author's life, the *Pieta, Signore.*

At the first vibration of that angelic voice, Hoffmann stood as if turned to stone, while old Gottlieb, gently lifting his daughter from his knees, deposited her, recumbent as she was, upon the couch; then, running to his Antonio Amati, he began to accompany her, producing with his bow an undercurrent of harmony, and supporting Antonia's song as the angel supports the soul he carries up to heaven.

Antonia's voice was a soprano, possessing the greatest range that the divine lavishness can bestow, not upon a woman's but upon an angel's voice. Antonia's range was five octaves and a half; she could sing with equal facility high *C*, that divine note which seems adapted to none but celestial concerts, and the *C* of the fifth octave of low notes. Hoffmann had never heard anything of such velvet-like softness as the first four measures, sung without accompaniment, *Pieta, Signore, di me dolente.* That aspiration of the suffering soul Godward, that fervent prayer to the Lord to take pity on the suffering that found voice to lament, assumed in Antonia's mouth an accent of divine respect that resembled terror. The accompaniment too, which had taken up the phrase as it floated between heaven and earth, which had, so to speak, caught it in its arms after the *la* had died away, and which repeated the lament *piano, piano,* like an echo, — the accompaniment was in every way worthy of the heart-broken voice, and as sorrowful. It said, not in Italian, not in German, not in French, but in the universal tongue called music: —

"Have pity, O Lord, have pity on me, miserable creature that I am! Have pity, O Lord, and if my prayer reaches Thine ear, may Thy rigor be disarmed and may Thy glance be less stern and more merciful as it is turned upon me!"

And nevertheless, while following, while forming a frame, as it were, for the voice, the accompaniment left it all its liberty, all its fulness. It was a caress, not an embrace, a support and not an embarrassment; and when, at the first *sforzando*, when the voice rose to the *re* and the two *fas* as if to try to ascend to heaven, then the accompaniment seemed to fear burdening it as an earthly thing, and almost abandoned it to the wings of faith, only coming to its support on the *mi* sharp, that is to say, on the *diminuendo*, when, wearied by its effort, the voice fell back as if exhausted, like Canova's Madonna, on her knees, sitting upon her knees, in whom everything seems to bend, soul and body alike, crushed beneath the terrible fear that the Creator's pity will not be sufficiently great to forget the fault of His creature.

And when, in a tremulous voice, she continued: "May I never be damned and hurled into the everlasting fire of Thy rigor, O Almighty God!" then the accompaniment ventured to mingle with the trembling voice which, seeing the ever burning flames from afar, besought the Lord to turn them aside. Thereupon, the accompaniment in its turn prayed, implored, groaned, ascended with the voice to the *fa*, descended with it to the *do*, accompanying it in its weakness, sustaining it in its terror; and then, when the voice, gasping and nerveless, died in Antonia's chest, the accompaniment continued alone, as the prayers of the survivors, plaintive and murmuring, continue after the soul has flown and is already on the way to heaven.

At that moment the supplicating tones of Master Gottlieb's violin were reenforced by an unexpected burst of melody, at once sweet and powerful, almost divine. Antonia raised herself upon her elbow; Master Gottlieb turned half round and stood with his bow suspended over the strings of his violin. Hoffmann, who was at first dazed, intoxicated, delirious with joy, had realized that that sorrowing heart needed a little hope, and that it would break if a divine ray did not afford it a glimpse of heaven, and he had rushed to an organ and spread his ten fingers over the shuddering keys, and the organ, heaving a deep sigh, had mingled its notes with Gottlieb's violin and Antonia's voice.

A marvellous thing was the repetition of the *Pieta*, *Signore* motif, accompanied by that voice of hope, and not pursued by terror as in the first part; and when, with full faith in her genius as in her prayer, Antonia attacked the *fa* of the *volgi* with the whole power of her voice, a shudder ran through old Gottlieb's veins, and a cry escaped from Hoffmann's lips, as, drowning the Antonio Amati beneath the torrents of melody poured forth by the organ, he continued Antonia's voice after it had died away, and upon the wings, no longer of an angel, but of a tempest, seemed to carry that soul's last sigh to the feet of the Almighty and All-Merciful God.

Then there was a moment's silence; the three looked at one another, and their hands met in a fraternal grasp as their souls had met in a common harmony.

And from that moment, not only did Antonia call Hoffmann her brother, but old Gottlieb Murr called him his son.

VI.

THE OATH.

PERHAPS the reader will ask himself, or rather will ask us, how it happened that, Antonia's mother having died because of her singing, Master Gottlieb Murr permitted his daughter, that heart of his heart, to run the risk of a danger similar to that to which her mother had succumbed.

And in the beginning, when he heard Antonia try her first song, the poor father had trembled like the leaf upon which a bird perches while he sings. But Antonia was a veritable bird, and the old musician soon discovered that song was her natural language. And God, by bestowing upon her a voice of such range that it had not perhaps its equal in the world, had signified that Master Gottlieb had nothing to fear in that direction at all events; indeed, when that natural gift of song was reenforced by musical study, when the most complicated difficulties of the scale had been placed before the girl and overcome instantly with wonderful facility, without distortion of the features, without effort, without causing a single chord to show in her neck, without so much as a contraction of the eyes, he realized the perfection of the instrument; and as Antonia, even when singing pieces written for the highest voices, was never required to do her best, he was convinced that there was no danger in allowing the sweet-voiced nightingale to follow the bent of her melodious calling.

But Master Gottlieb had forgotten that the musical chord is not the only one that resounds in a maiden's heart, and that there is another one much more fragile, more easily played upon, and more deadly,— the chord of love!

That chord waked in the poor child's heart at the first note produced by Hoffmann's bow. Bending over her embroidery in the room adjoining that in which the young and the old man were, she had raised her head at the first shuddering sound that passed through the air. She had listened; then little by little a strange sensation had crept into her heart, had glided through her veins in unfamiliar thrills. She had risen slowly to her feet, resting one hand on her chair, while the other dropped the embroidery from its open fingers. She had stood for an instant without moving; then she had walked slowly toward the door and had appeared, as we have said, the shadow of material life, a poetic vision, at the door of Master Gottlieb's study.

We have seen how music had blended those three souls into a single one in its white-hot crucible, and how, at the end of the concert, Hoffmann had become as one of the family.

It was the hour at which old Gottlieb was accustomed to dine. He invited Hoffmann to dine with him, and the invitation was accepted with the same cordiality with which it was given.

Thereupon for a few moments the lovely and poetic virgin of the divine aria was transformed into an excellent housekeeper. Antonia poured tea like Clarissa Harlowe, spread the butter on slices of bread like Charlotte, and ended by taking her seat at the table and eating like an ordinary mortal.

The Germans do not understand poetry as we do. According to the theory of our self-conscious society, the woman who eats and drinks loses the poetic glamor. If

a young and pretty woman sits at the table, it is only to
preside over the repast; if she has a glass in front of her,
it is to put her gloves in, unless, indeed, she keeps her
gloves on her hands; if she has a plate, it is to hold a
bunch of grapes, of which the immaterial creature conde-
scends to suck a few of the finest at the close of the feast,
as a bee sucks a flower.

The reader will understand that, after the welcome
Hoffmann had received at Master Gottlieb's, he went
again the next day and the next and every day thereafter.
As far as Master Gottlieb was concerned, the frequency
of Hoffmann's visits did not seem to disturb him.   Antonia was too pure, too chaste, she trusted her father too
fully, for the old man to harbor a suspicion that she
could commit a sin. His daughter was to him as Saint
Cecilia, the Virgin Mary, an angel from heaven; the
divine essence in her was so pre-eminent over earthly
substance, that the old man had never thought it necessary to tell her that there is more danger in the contact
of two bodies than in the union of two souls.

So Hoffmann was happy, as happy, that is to say, as
it is given to a mortal creature to be. The sun of joy
never illumines every corner of a man's heart; there is
always, at some point or other, a dark spot that reminds
man that absolute happiness does not exist in this world,
but only in heaven.

But Hoffmann had one advantage over the great ma-
jority of his kind. It often happens that a man cannot
define the cause of the sorrow that assails him in the
midst of his happiness, the shadow that falls, dark and
ominous, upon his radiant felicity.

Now Hoffmann knew what it was that marred his
happiness.

It was the promise he had made Zacharias Werner to

join him in Paris; it was that strange longing to visit France, which vanished as soon as Hoffmann was in Antonia's presence, but regained the upper hand as soon as he was alone; more than that, as time passed and Zacharias' letters, reminding his friend of his promise, became more urgent, Hoffmann became more melancholy.

At last the young girl's presence was no longer sufficient to drive away the phantom that haunted Hoffmann thenceforth, even when he was at Antonia's side. Often, when he was with her, he fell into a deep reverie. Of what was he dreaming? of Zacharias Werner, whose voice he seemed to hear. Often his eye, after wandering vaguely about, seemed to rest upon a certain point on the horizon. What did that eye see, or rather, what did it fancy that it saw? The road to Paris, and at one of the turns in the road Zacharias walking before him and motioning to him to follow.

Gradually, the phantom that had at first appeared to Hoffmann at rare and unequal intervals, returned with more regularity, and at last haunted him from morning till night.

Hoffmann fell deeper and deeper in love with Antonia. He felt that Antonia was necessary to his life, that she was his only hope of future happiness; but he felt, too, that before entering upon that happiness, and to make sure that it would be enduring, he must carry out the pilgrimage he had planned; for otherwise the desire confined in his heart, strange as it might appear, would gnaw constantly at it.

One day, as he sat beside Antonia while Master Gottlieb in his cabinet was copying the score of Pergolese's "Stabat," which he proposed to perform at the Frankfort Philharmonic Society, Hoffmann fell into one of his cus-

tomary fits of musing. Antonia, after watching him for
a long while, took both his hands in hers.

"You must go there, my friend," she said.

Hoffmann stared at her in amazement.

"Go there?" he repeated; "where, pray?"

"To France, to Paris."

"Who told you, Antonia, of that secret thought of my
heart, which I dare not confess to myself?"

"I might claim to possess the power of a fairy, Theodor, and say to you, 'I have read your thoughts, I have
read your eyes, I have read your heart;' but I should
say what is not true. No, I remember, that is all."

"And what do you remember, my beloved Antonia?"

"I remember that on the day before you first came
here, Zacharias Werner came and told us of your pro-
jected journey, your ardent desire to see Paris; a desire
cherished for more than a year, and on the point of being
gratified. Since then you have told me what prevented
you from going. You have told me that, on seeing me
for the first time, you were seized by that irresistible
feeling by which I was myself seized when I listened to
your playing, and now it only remains for you to tell me
this: that you still love me as dearly."

Hoffmann made a gesture.

"Do not take the trouble to tell me," continued Antonia; "I know that you do; but there is something
even stronger than your love, and that is your longing to
go to France, to join Zacharias, to see Paris, in fact."

"Antonia!" cried Hoffmann, "all that you say is
true, with the exception of one point : that is, that there
is anything on earth stronger than my love! No, Antonia, I swear to you that that longing — a strange longing which I do not understand — I should have buried
in my heart if you had not drawn it forth yourself. You

are not mistaken, Antonia! There is a voice that summons me to Paris, a voice stronger than my will, and yet, I say again, I should not have heeded it, — that voice is the voice of destiny ! "

"Very well, let us fulfil our destiny, my friend. You shall go to-morrow. How much time do you want ? "

"A month, Antonia; in a month I shall return."

"A month will not be enough for you, Theodor; in a month you will have seen nothing. I give you two months; I give you three months; I give you all the time you want, in short; but I demand one thing, or rather, two things of you."

"What are they, dear Antonia ? What are they ? tell me quickly."

"To-morrow will be Sunday, the day when high mass is celebrated. Look out of your window as you did on the day that Zacharias Werner went away, and you will see me go up the church steps as on that day, my dear, only more sad than then. Come and join me in my usual place; come and sit beside me, and at the moment when the priest blesses our Lord's blood, you must take two oaths, — one, to remain true to me; the other, not to gamble any more."

"Oh! whatever you wish, on the spot, dear Antonia; I swear — "

"Nay, Theodor, you shall swear to-morrow."

"Antonia, Antonia, you are an angel ! "

"As we are about to part, Theodor, have you not something to say to my father ? "

"Yes, you are right. But I confess, Antonia, that I hesitate, I tremble. Great God ! who am I that I dare to hope — "

"You are the man I love, Theodor. Go and speak to my father, go."

She waved her hand to Hoffmann, and opened the door leading to a small room used by her as an oratory.

Hoffmann looked until the door had closed, and sent to her through the door all the outpourings of his heart, with all the kisses of his lips.

Then he entered Master Gottlieb's study.

Master Gottlieb was so accustomed to Hoffmann's footsteps, that he did not even take his eyes from the desk on which he was copying the "Stabat." The young man entered and stood behind him.

After a moment, as he heard nothing more, not even the young man's breathing, Master Gottlieb turned.

"Ah! is it you, boy?" he said, throwing back his head so that he could see Hoffmann through his spectacles. "What have you to say to me?"

Hoffmann opened his mouth, but he closed it again without having uttered a sound.

"Have you gone dumb?" asked the old man. "Bless my soul! that would be a pity. A rascal who uses his voice as you do when you set about it, can't lose it like that, unless by way of punishment for having abused it!"

"No, Master Gottlieb, no, I have n't lost my voice, thank God! But, what I have to say to you—"

"Well?"

"Why, it seems to me rather hard to say."

"Bah! is it such a very hard thing to say: 'Master Gottlieb, I love your daughter?'"

"You know that, Master Gottlieb?"

"Upon my word! I must have been a great fool, or rather a great stupid, not to have discovered your love."

"And yet you have allowed me to go on loving her."

"Why not? as she loves you."

"But you know that I have no fortune, Master Gottlieb."

"Pshaw! have the birds of the air a fortune? They sing, they mate, they build a nest, and God feeds them. We artists much resemble birds; we sing, and God comes to our aid. When the singing is not sufficient, you will be a painter; when the painting is not sufficient, you will be a musician. I was no richer than you when I married my poor Teresa; but we never were without bread or a roof to shelter us. I have always needed money, and I have never failed to get it. Are you rich in love? that is all I ask you. Are you worthy of the treasure you covet? that is all I want to know. Do you love Antonia better than your life, better than your soul? If you do, my mind is at rest; Antonia will never lack anything. If you do not love her, that is a different matter; though you have a hundred thousand thalers a year, she will always lack everything."

Hoffmann was ready to kneel before the artist's beautiful philosophy. He bent over the old man's hand, and the old man drew him to his side and embraced him.

"Well, well," he said, "it is settled. Take your journey, as you are tormented by the wild longing to hear the horrible music of Monsieur Méhul and Monsieur Dalayrac; it's a young man's disease that will soon be cured. I have no fear; take your journey, my dear boy, and come back to us. You will find Mozart here and Beethoven, Cimarosa, Pergolese, Paesiello, Porpora, and, in addition, Master Gottlieb and his daughter; that is to say, a father and a wife. Go, my child, go."

And Master Gottlieb once more embraced Hoffmann, who, seeing that night was approaching, realized that he had no time to lose, and went home to make preparations for his departure.

The next morning early, Hoffmann was at his window. As the time for leaving Antonia drew near, the separation seemed more and more impossible to him. The whole delightful period of his life that had just passed, the seven months which had flown by like a single day, and which appeared in his memory, now like a vast horizon which he embraced at a single glance, and again like a series of happy days, flitting by one after another, smiling and crowned with flowers; Antonia's sweet songs, which had formed an atmosphere about him thickly sown with delicious melodies,—all this was such a potent attraction that it struggled, almost successfully, with the unknown, that wonderful wizard, who attracts the strongest, the least emotional hearts.

At ten o'clock Antonia appeared at the corner of the street, where, seven months before, Hoffmann had seen her for the first time. Her maid Lisbeth followed her as usual, and they went up the church steps. On the top step Antonia turned, saw Hoffmann, summoned him with a motion of her hand, and entered the church.

Hoffmann rushed out of the house and entered the church. Antonia was already kneeling and in prayer.

Hoffmann was a Protestant, and the chanting in a foreign tongue had always seemed most absurd to him; but when he heard Antonia's voice soaring upward in the church music that is at once so soft and so majestic, he was sorry that he did not know the words, so that he might join his voice to hers, which was made even sweeter by the profound melancholy under which she was laboring.

Throughout the celebration of the mass she sang on, in the same voice in which the angels in heaven sing. And when the choir boy's bell announced the consecration of the host, when the faithful bowed their heads before the God who rose above their heads in the priest's hands, Antonia alone raised her head.

"Swear," she said.

"I swear," said Hoffmann, in a trembling voice, "I swear to give up gambling."

"Is that the only oath you intend to take, my friend?"

"Oh, no! wait. I swear to remain true to you in heart and mind, in body and soul."

"Upon what do you swear it?"

"Oh!" cried Hoffmann, in intense excitement, "I swear it upon what I hold most dear and most sacred, upon your life!"

"Thanks!" cried Antonia. "For if you do not keep your oath, I shall die."

Hoffmann started, a shudder ran through his body; he did not regret what he had done, but he was afraid.

The priest descended the steps of the altar, carrying the blessed sacrament in the host.

As the divine body of Our Lord passed by, she seized Hoffmann's hand.

"You heard his oath, did you not, O God?" she said.

Hoffmann essayed to speak.

"Not another word, not one; I propose that the words of your oath, being the last I have heard from your lips, shall ring forever in my ears. *Auf wiederseh'n*, my dear, *auf wiederseh'n*."

The girl glided away, light as a shadow, leaving a locket in her lover's hand. Hoffmann looked after her as Orpheus must have looked after the fleeing Eurydice. When she had disappeared, he opened the locket.

It contained a portrait of Antonia, resplendent with youth and beauty.

Two hours later Hoffmann took his place in the same diligence Zacharias Werner had taken, saying to himself, —

"Never fear, Antonia. Ah! no, I will not gamble! Ah! yes, I will be true to you!"

VII.

A PARIS BARRIER IN 1793.

THE young man's journey through the France he had so longed to see was melancholy enough. It was not that he experienced so many difficulties on approaching the centre as he would have met with had he been going to the frontier. No, the French Republic welcomed the coming more warmly than it sped the parting guest.

However, a stranger was not admitted to the honor of enjoying the benefits of that precious form of government until he had complied with certain formalities that were none too mild.

It was the period when the French knew least about writing, but when they wrote more than ever before. It seemed meet, therefore, to all recently appointed functionaries to abandon their domestic or mechanical callings, in order to sign and visa passports, draw up descriptions, invite recommendations, and, in a word, to do whatever befits the profession of patriot.

The paper trade had never been so flourishing as at that period. That endemic disease of the French people, being grafted upon terrorism, produced the finest specimens of grotesque calligraphy that had ever been heard of up to that time.

Hoffmann's passport was remarkably small. It was the day of small things. Newspapers, books, the pamphlets hawked about the streets were all reduced to the simple octavo at the largest. But, small as it was, the traveller's passport was invaded as soon as he entered Alsace, by official signatures which were not unlike the zigzags described by a drunken man as he staggers diagonally across the street, colliding with both walls.

Hoffmann was compelled, therefore, to add one leaf to his passport there, and another in Lorraine, where the handwritings assumed especially colossal proportions. Where patriotism was hottest, the writers were most artless. There was one mayor, who filled two pages, back and front, with an autograph memorandum thus conceived: —

"Auphemann, chune Allemans, ami de la liberté, se rendan à Pari ha pié.

"Signé: GOLIER."[1]

Armed with that document, giving the above full particulars concerning his native country, his age, his principles, his destination, and his means of transport, Hoffmann's only preoccupation was to sew all those civic fragments together, and we should say that when he reached Paris he had a very respectable volume, which, he said, he proposed to have bound in tin if he should ever undertake another journey, because, as he was compelled to keep the sheets constantly in his hand, they ran too great a risk in a simple pasteboard cover.

Everywhere these or similar words were repeated to him: —

"My dear traveller, the provinces are still habitable, but Paris is in a very excited state. Be on your guard,

---

[1] Hoffmann, jeune Allemand, ami de la liberté, se rendant à Paris à pied.

Hoffmann, a young German, friend of liberty, on his way to Paris on foot.

citizen, they have a very captious police force in Paris, and, being a German, you may not be treated like a good Frenchman."

To which Hoffmann replied with a proud smile, reminiscent of the proud bearing of the Spartans when the Thessalian spies tried to exaggerate the forces of Xerxes, King of the Persians.

He arrived before Paris. It was evening, and the barriers were closed.

Hoffmann spoke French fairly well, but a man is a German or he is not. If he is not a German he may have an accent which after a while will pass for the accent of one of our provinces. If he is a German, he is always known for a German.

We must explain how police duty was done at the barriers.

In the first place they were closed. Then seven or eight sectionaries, shrewd and intelligent idlers, amateur Lavaters, smoking their pipes, prowled around in squads, in attendance upon two or three agents of the municipal police.

Those worthy fellows, who, passing from one service to another, had ended by haunting all the clubs, all the district bureaux, all the places into which politics had crept in an active or a passive sense; who had seen every deputy at the National Assembly or the Convention, all the aristocrats, male and female, in the galleries, all the notorious dandies on the boulevards, all the suspected celebrities at the theatres, all the prisoners, whether convicted or discharged, in the courts, and all the respited priests in the prisons, — those worthy patriots knew their Paris so well that every familiar face was likely to impress them as it passed, and, we may say, almost invariably did so impress them.

16

It was no simple matter to disguise one's self in those days. Too much magnificence in the costume caught the eye, too great simplicity aroused suspicion. As uncleanliness was one of the most popular insignia of true civism, every water-carrier, every scullion might conceal an aristocrat; and then, how could the white hand with the beautiful nails be entirely disguised. And that aristocratic gait, which is the simplest of all gaits in our day, when the lowliest wear the highest heels, — how conceal it from twenty pairs of eyes keener than the nose of the bloodhound following a trail?

A traveller was therefore, immediately upon his arrival, searched, questioned, stripped bare, morally speaking, with a facility born of practice, and a liberty born of — liberty.

Hoffmann appeared before that tribunal about six o'clock in the evening of December 7. The weather was dull and disagreeable, a mixture of fog and sleet; but the bearskin and otter skin caps that imprisoned the patriot heads kept so much warm blood in their brains and their ears that they were in full possession of their presence of mind and their unexcelled faculties of investigation.

Hoffmann was stopped by a hand placed lightly on his breast.

The young traveller was dressed in an iron-gray coat and a heavy overcoat, and his German boots outlined a very shapely leg. He had encountered no mud since the last post-house, although the post-chaise had been unable to go on because of the sleet, and Hoffmann had done six leagues on foot, over a road thinly covered with frozen snow.

" Where are you going, citizen, with your fine boots ? " said a police agent to the young man.

"I am going to Paris, citizen."

"You take a good deal for granted, my young *Prusssssian*," rejoined the sectionary, pronouncing the word with a prodigality of *s*'s which attracted the attention of half a score of idlers to the traveller.

The Prussians were at that moment as great foes to France as the Philistines were to the compatriots of Samson the Israelite.

"Well, yes, I am a *Pruzian*," retorted Hoffmann, changing the sectionary's five *s*'s into a *z*. "What then?"

"Why, if you're a Prussian, you're a little spy of Pitt and Cobourg, eh?"

"Read my passports," said Hoffmann, exhibiting his volume to one of the scholars of the barrier.

"Come," replied the man addressed, turning on his heel to escort the stranger to the guard-house.

Hoffmann followed his guide with perfect tranquillity.

When, by the light of the smoking candles, the patriots saw the nervous youth, with steadfast eye and disordered hair, hammering at his French with the utmost conscientiousness, one of them cried, —

"He won't deny that he's an aristocrat. See what hands and feet he has!"

"You're a fool, citizen," retorted Hoffmann. "I'm as good a patriot as you, and what's more, I'm an artist."

As he spoke he drew from his pocket one of those appallingly huge pipes, of which a German diver alone can find the bottom.

The pipe produced a prodigious effect upon the sectionaries, who were smoking their tobacco in miniature vessels.

They all gazed wonderingly at the young man as he

packed into his pipe, with a dexterity born of long practice, enough tobacco to last them a week.

Then he sat down, patiently held a light to the tobacco until there was a great crust of fire on the surface of the bowl, and expelled at regular intervals dense clouds of smoke, which emerged in graceful bluish columns from his nose and his lips.

" He smokes well," said one of the sectionaries.

" And it seems that he 's a famous fellow," said another. " Just look at his certificates."

" What have you come to Paris for ? " asked a third.

" To study the science of liberty," replied Hoffmann.

" And what else ? " continued the Frenchman, little affected by the heroic ring of the phrase, probably because he had heard it so much.

" And painting," said Hoffmann.

" Ah! you 're a painter, like Citizen David, are you ? "

" Exactly."

" Do you know how to paint Roman patriots, all naked, as he does ? "

" I paint them all dressed," Hoffmann replied.

" They 're not so fine that way."

" That depends," said Hoffmann with imperturbable *sang froid.*

" Do my portrait," said the sectionary admiringly.

" I will gladly do it."

Hoffmann took a burning brand from the stove, waited until the glowing end had cooled, then drew upon the whitewashed wall one of the ugliest faces that ever dishonored the capital of the civilized world.

The fur cap and fox's tail, the driveling mouth, the thick whiskers, the short pipe, the retreating chin, were copied with such rare fidelity to truth, that the whole of the guard on duty requested the favor of having their portraits done by the young man.

Hoffmann granted their requests with good grace, and sketched on the wall a series of patriots, quite as successfully executed but less noble, most assuredly, than the bourgeois in Rembrandt's "Ronde Nocturne."

When he had once put the patriots in good humor, there was no further question of suspicion. The German was a naturalized Parisian. They offered him beer, and he, like the thoughtful youth he was, offered his hosts Burgundy, which they accepted with the greatest cordiality.

Then it was that one of them, more cunning than the others, took his thick nose in the hook of his forefinger, and said to Hoffmann with a wink of his left eye, —

"Tell us one thing, Citizen German."

"What is it, my friend?"

"Tell us the object of your journey."

"I have told you: politics and painting."

"No, no, something else."

"I assure you, citizen — "

"You understand, of course, that we sha'n't make any charges against you. We like you, and we 'll protect you; but there are two delegates here from the Cordeliers Club and two from the Jacobins. I myself belong to the Brothers and Friends. Select among us the club to which you prefer to do homage."

"Homage, what do you mean?" said Hoffmann, greatly surprised.

"Oh! don't try to hide it. It's such a fine thing that you ought to display it everywhere."

"Really, citizen, you make me blush; explain yourself."

"Look and tell me if I am not good at guessing."

He opened the book of passports and pointed with his fat finger to the following lines under the heading of Strasburg:—

"Hoffmann, travelling from Mannheim, had in his possession at Strasburg a box marked thus: O. B."

"That is true," said Hoffmann.

"Very good! what does that box contain?"

"I declared its contents to the customs officers at Strasburg."

"Just see, citizens, what this sly dog is bringing here. You remember what our patriots at Auxerre sent us?"

"Yes," said one; "a box of lard."

"What for?"

"To grease the guillotine," cried a number of well-satisfied voices.

"Well!" said Hoffmann, changing color a little, "what connection can there be between this box of mine and the box sent by the patriots of Auxerre?"

"Read," said the Parisian, pointing to his passport. "Read, young man: 'Travelling for politics and art.' It is written!"

"O Republic!" muttered Hoffmann.

"So confess, young friend of liberty," said his protector.

"That would be taking credit for an idea that never occurred to me," replied Hoffmann. "I don't care for false glory. No, the box I had at Strasburg, which will arrive by carrier, contains only a violin, a box of colors, and some rolls of canvas."

Those words caused a great diminution in the esteem which some of those present had conceived for Hoffmann. They gave him back his papers. They drank bumpers with him, but they ceased to look upon him as the saviour of enslaved nations.

One of the patriots went so far as to remark, —

"He looks like Saint-Just, but I prefer Saint-Just."

Hoffmann, once more buried in his reverie, which the heat of the stove, the tobacco, and the Burgundy tended to deepen, sat for some time without speaking. But suddenly he raised his head.

"Is the guillotine doing a good deal of work here?" he asked.

"Pretty well, pretty well. It's fallen off a little since the Brissotins, but still it's very satisfactory."

"Do you know where I can find comfortable lodgings, my friends?"

"Anywhere."

"But where I can see everything."

"Ah! in that case you must find a place in the neighborhood of Quai aux Fleurs."

"Very good."

"Do you know where Quai aux Fleurs is?"

"No, but the word *fleurs* [flowers] pleases me. I fancy myself already installed on Quai aux Fleurs. How do I get there?"

"You must go straight down Rue d'Enfer, and you'll get to the quay."

"Quay, that means that it's on the water!" said Hoffmann.

"Exactly."

"And that water is the Seine?"

"The Seine."

"So the Quai aux Fleurs is on the Seine, is it?"

"You know Paris better than I do, Citizen German."

"Thanks. Farewell. May I go in?"

"You have one more little formality to comply with."

" What is that? "

" You must go to the commissioner of police and get from him a permit to stay in the city."

" Very good! Farewell."

" Wait a moment. With that permit from the commissioner you must go to the police."

" Oho! "

" And give the address of your lodgings."

" Very good! is that all? "

"No; you must go to the headquarters of the section."

" What for? "

" To satisfy the authorities as to your means of subsistence."

" I will do all that; and will that be all? "

" Not yet. You will have to show your patriotism by gifts."

" Willingly."

" And take an oath of hatred to all French and foreign tyrants."

" With all my heart. Thanks for your valuable information."

" And then you must n't forget to write your full name legibly on a placard and hang it at your door."

" That shall be done."

" Go now, citizen, you annoy us."

The bottles were empty.

" Farewell, citizens. Many thanks for your courtesy."

And Hoffmann took his leave, still accompanied by his pipe, which was burning more fiercely than ever.

That is how he made his entry into the capital of republican France.

The fascinating phrase, " Quai aux Fleurs," had made his mouth water. He saw in his mind's eye a little room with a balcony, looking on that marvellous Quai aux Fleurs.

He forgot December and the north winds. He forgot the snow and the temporary death of all nature. The flowers bloomed in his imagination under the smoke that poured from his lips. He saw nothing but jasmine and roses, despite the filthy streets of the faubourg.

As the clock struck nine, he reached Quai aux Fleurs, which was as utterly dark and deserted as all the northern quays are in winter. But that evening the solitude was darker and more noticeable there than anywhere.

Hoffmann was too hungry and too cold to philosophize in the open air; but there was no public house on the quay.

Raising his eyes, he discovered at last, on the corner of the quay and Rue de la Barillerie, a common red lantern, within which a dirty wick flickered dimly.

That beacon light swung back and forth at the end of an iron bracket, very well adapted for the suspension of a political foe in those days of tumult.

Hoffmann saw these words in green letters on the red glass: —

"ROOMS TO LET. — FURNISHED BEDROOMS AND CABINETS."

He knocked sharply at a hall door. The door opened; the traveller entered, feeling his way.

"Shut your door," cried a harsh voice.

And a huge dog barked, as if to say, —

"Look out for your legs!"

Having agreed as to terms with a landlady of not unattractive aspect, and having selected his room, Hoffmann found himself in possession of a space fifteen feet by eight, forming a bedroom and study in one, at a rent of thirty sous per day, payable every morning when he rose.

Hoffmann was in such high spirits that he paid for a fortnight in advance, for fear that some one might undertake to deprive him of his precious lodgings.

That done, he went to bed between sheets that were decidedly damp; but any bed is a bed to a traveller of eighteen. And then, too, how could he be exacting when he had the good fortune to lodge on Quai aux Fleurs?

Moreover Hoffmann invoked the memory of Antonia, and is not the place where one invokes the angels always paradise?

VIII.

**HOW THE MUSEUMS AND LIBRARIES WERE CLOSED,
BUT PLACE DE LA RÉVOLUTION WAS OPEN.**

THE room which was destined to be Hoffmann's terrestrial paradise for a fortnight contained a bed, as we know, a table, and two chairs.

It had a mantel-piece embellished with two blue glass vases filled with artificial flowers. A figure of Liberty in sugar posed beneath a crystal bell in which its tricolored flag and red cap were reflected.

A copper chandelier, a corner-piece in old rosewood, a twelfth century tapestry for a curtain, — such was the furniture of the apartment as disclosed by the first rays of dawn.

The tapestry represented Orpheus playing the violin to win back Eurydice, and the violin naturally recalled Zacharias Werner to Hoffmann's memory.

" Dear friend," mused our traveller, " he is in Paris, and so am I. We are together, and I shall see him to-day or to-morrow at latest. Where shall I begin? How must I set to work in order not to waste any of the good Lord's time and to see everything in France? For several days past I have seen nothing but living pictures, and very ugly ones at that. Let's go to the ex-tyrant's Louvre. There I shall see all the fine pictures he had, the Rubens, the Poussins. Let's be off at once."

He rose and went to the window, to examine first the panoramic tableau of his neighborhood.

A dull, gray sky, black mud under white trees, people running busily hither and thither, and a noise like the murmur of running water. That is all he discovered.

There was but little that was suggestive of flowers. Hoffmann closed his window, breakfasted, and went out, proposing first of all to see his friend Zacharias Werner.

But, as he was on the point of starting, he remembered that Werner had never given him his address, without which it would be somewhat difficult to find him.

That was no small disappointment to Hoffmann. But in a moment he said to himself, —

"Fool that I am! Zacharias loves the same things that I do. I long to see fine paintings. He must have had the same longing. I shall find him or some trace of him at the Louvre. Let us go to the Louvre."

He could see the Louvre from the parapet of the quay, so he bent his steps in the direction of the pile.

But he was grieved to learn at the door that the French, since they had been free, did not choose to debase themselves by looking at paintings of slaves, and that, assuming, which was not probable, that the Commune of Paris had not already burned up all the daubs to feed the fires in the manufactories of weapons of war, they would take care to use all that oil to feed the rats that were destined to furnish the patriots with food when the Prussians should lay siege to Paris.

Hoffmann felt the perspiration start on his forehead. The man who spoke thus to him had a certain manner of speaking that betrayed his importance.

The eloquent orator was much applauded.

Hoffmann learned from one of the bystanders that he had the honor of speaking to Citizen Simon, governor of the *children of France* and curator of the royal museums.

"I shall not see any pictures," he said with a sigh. "Ah me! it's a great pity! But I will go to the late king's Library, and, in lieu of pictures, I shall see there engravings, medals, and manuscripts. I shall see the tomb of Childeric, Clovis' father, and Père Coronelli's celestial and terrestrial globes."

But Hoffmann, when he reached the Library, was pained to learn that the French nation, looking upon science and literature as a source of corruption and bad citizenship, had closed all the places of resort of pretended scholars and pretended men of letters, from motives of humanity, and to save themselves the trouble of guillotining the poor devils. Moreover, even under the tyrant, the Library was open only twice a week.

Hoffmann was obliged to retire without seeing anything. He even forgot to ask for news of his friend Zacharias.

But, as he was a persevering youth, he persisted in his efforts, and tried to gain admission to the Sainte-Avoye Museum. He was informed that the proprietor had been guillotined two days before.

He went as far as the Luxembourg; but that palace had become a prison.

His strength and his courage being alike exhausted, he retraced his steps toward his hotel, to rest his weary legs a little, to dream of Antonia and Zacharias, and to smoke a two hours' pipe in solitude.

But, marvel of marvels! That same Quai aux Fleurs, recently so peaceful, so deserted, was black with a multitude of people, rushing about and shouting discordantly.

Hoffmann, who was not tall, could see nothing over the shoulders of all those people. He made haste to force his way through the crowd with his sharp elbows, and to return to his room.

He stationed himself at his window.

All eyes were at once turned upon him, and he was embarrassed for a moment, for he noticed how few windows were open. However, the curiosity of the crowd was soon directed to some other point than Hoffmann's window, and the young man himself did as the others did, and looked at the porch of a great black building with pointed roofs, and a belfry at the top of a large square tower.

He summoned the landlady.

" Citizeness," he said, " what is that building, pray ? "

" The Palais, citizen."

" What do they do at the Palais ? "

" They try people at the Palais de Justice, citizen."

" I thought there were no courts now."

" Oh ! yes, there 's the Revolutionary Tribunal."

" Ah ! true — and all these good people ? "

" Are waiting for the arrival of the tumbrils."

" What ? the tumbrils ? I don't quite understand. Excuse me, I am a foreigner."

" The tumbrils, citizen, are just the same as hearses for dead people."

" Ah ! Gott im Himmel ! "

" Yes; in the morning the prisoners arrive who are to be tried by the Revolutionary Tribunal."

" I see."

" At four o'clock the prisoners are all tried, and they

pack them in the tumbrils that Citizen Fouquier has ordered for that purpose."

"Who is Citizen Fouquier?"

"The public prosecutor."

"Very well, and then?"

"Then the tumbrils go at a slow trot to Place de la Révolution, where the guillotine stands all the time."

"Really!"

"What! you have been out and you didn't go to see the guillotine? That's the first thing strangers go to see when they arrive. It seems that we French are the only people who have guillotines."

"I congratulate you, madame."

"Say citizeness."

"I beg your pardon."

"Look, the tumbrils are coming — "

"You are going, citizeness?"

"Yes, I no longer like to see it."

And the landlady moved away.

Hoffmann laid his hand gently on her arm.

"Excuse me if I ask you one question," he said.

"Ask it."

"Why do you say you *no longer* like to see it? For my part, I should have said, ' I *do not* like to see it.' "

"This is how it is, citizen. At first they guillotined wicked aristocrats, it seems. Those people carried their heads so high, and they all had such an insolent, insulting way about them that pity didn't moisten our eyes very readily. So we looked on willingly enough. It was a fine sight to see the struggle of those bold enemies of the nation against death. But one day I saw an old man on the tumbril with his head jolting against the slats. It was a sad sight. The next day I saw some nuns. Another day I saw a child of fourteen, and last

of all I saw a girl in one tumbril and her mother in
another, and the two poor creatures throwing kisses to
each other without a word. They were so pale, their
expression was so sad, the smile on their lips so ghastly,
the fingers, which were the only part of them that moved
as they took the kisses from their mouths, were so white
and trembled so, that I shall never forget the horrid
sight, and I have sworn never to run the risk of seeing
such another."

"Oho!" said Hoffmann, moving away from the
window, "do they do such things as that?"

"Yes, citizen. Why, what are you doing?"

"Closing the window."

"What for?"

"So as not to see."

"You! a man!"

"You see, citizeness, I came to Paris to study art and
to breathe the air of liberty. Now, if I should have
the ill-fortune to see such a sight as you just described,
if I should see a young girl or a woman being dragged
to her death, although longing to live, I should think
of my sweetheart, citizeness, whom I love dearly, and
who perhaps — no, citizeness, I will stay no longer in
this room. Haven't you one on the back of the
house?"

"Hush! foolish man, you speak too loud. Suppose
my officials should hear you?"

"Your officials! what do you mean by officials?"

"It's the republican name for servant."

"Well! if your servants should hear me, what would
happen?"

"It would happen that, three or four days hence, I
might see you from this window, in one of the tumbrils,
at half-past four in the afternoon."

Having uttered these words in a mysterious tone, the good woman ran hastily downstairs, and Hoffmann followed her.

He glided out of the house, resolved to do anything to avoid the popular spectacle.

When he was at the corner of the quay, the sabres of the gendarmes gleamed in the air; there was a movement in the crowd; the dense masses of people roared and began to run.

Hoffmann made his way at full speed to Rue Saint-Denis, and ran along that thoroughfare like a madman. He doubled on his tracks through various narrow streets, like a hare, and disappeared in the labyrinth of passages that run in all directions between Quai de la Ferraille and the markets.

He breathed freely at last, when he found himself on Rue de la Ferrourerie, where, with the keen insight of the poet and painter, he identified the spot made famous by the assassination of Henri IV.

From there he went on, looking about him in every direction, until he reached Rue Saint-Honoré. The shops were closed wherever he went. Hoffmann wondered at the tranquillity of the quarter. Not only were the shops closed, but the windows of certain houses were hermetically sealed, as if they had received a signal.

That state of things was soon explained to Hoffmann's satisfaction. He saw the cabs turn and take to the side streets. He heard the galloping of horses, and recognized the gendarmes; and behind them, in the evening mist, he saw a confused, ghastly hubbub of rags, arms waving in the air, pikes brandishing, and flaming eyes.

And above it all, a tumbril.

Issuing from that whirlwind, which burst upon him before he could fly or conceal himself, Hoffmann heard

17

such ear-piercing, piteous shrieks as never had fallen upon his ears until that evening.

On the tumbril was a woman dressed in white. Those shrieks issued from the lips, the soul, the whole distracted body of that woman.

Hoffmann felt his legs give way under him. Those piteous shrieks had deprived his nerves of all their force. He sank upon a stone, with his head resting against the shutters of a shop, which had been closed so hurriedly that they were still partly ajar.

The tumbril arrived opposite him, with its escort of bandits and hideous women, its usual satellites; but, strangely enough, all those dregs did not effervesce, all those reptiles made no sound. The victim alone writhed in the arms of two men, and called frantically upon heaven and earth, upon men and things.

Suddenly Hoffmann heard, through the chink in the shutters, these words pronounced in a sad tone by a sympathetic, youthful voice, —

"Poor Du Barry! so you have come to this!"

"Madame du Barry!" cried Hoffmann. "Is it she, is that she passing on the tumbril?"

"Yes, monsieur," replied the low, pitying voice in the traveller's ear, so close that he felt his interlocutor's hot breath between the boards.

Poor Du Barry was standing erect, clinging to the moving side of the tumbril. Her chestnut hair, the pride of her beauty, had been cut at the neck, but fell around the temples in long locks drenched with sweat. Lovely still, with her great, haggard eyes, her little mouth, — too small for the frightful outcry she was making, — the unhappy woman shook her head convulsively from time to time to throw aside the hair that covered her face.

When she passed the stone on which Hoffmann had fallen, she cried, "Help! save me! I have done no harm! help!" and she nearly overturned the executioner's assistant who was holding her.

That cry of "Help!" she did not cease to utter amid the profound silence of the multitude. Those furies, who were in the habit of heaping insults upon the victims who went bravely to their death, were touched by the irresistible outburst of a woman's terror. They felt that their outcries would not have succeeded in drowning the groans of that fever which bordered upon madness, and was sublime in its very horror.

Hoffmann rose, no longer conscious of a heart within his breast. He began to run after the tumbril with the rest, one more ghost added to the procession of spectres that formed the last escort of a king's favorite.

Madame du Barry noticed him and shrieked, —

"Life! life! I give all I own to the nation! Monsieur! Save me!"

"She spoke to me!" thought the young man. "Poor woman, whose glances were once valued so high, whose words were priceless treasures, she spoke to me!"

He halted. The tumbril had reached Place de la Révolution. In the darkness, increased by a cold rain, Hoffmann could see naught but two shadows: one, all white, was that of the victim; the other, red, of the scaffold.

He saw the executioners drag the white dress up the ladder. He saw that struggling form straighten itself out to resist, then suddenly, amid her piercing shrieks, the poor woman lost her balance and fell on the block.

Hoffmann heard her cry: "Mercy, Monsieur le Bourreau![1] Just one moment more, Monsieur le

---

[1] Executioner.

Bourreau!" And that was all. The knife fell with a
sinister flash.

Hoffmann fell backward into the ditch that surrounded the square.

It was a fine picture for an artist who had come to
France in search of impressions and ideas. God had
allowed him to witness the too cruel punishment of the
woman who had helped to destroy the monarchy.

La du Barry's cowardly death seemed to him to
absolve the poor creature. She could never have had
any pride, since she did not even know how to die!
To know how to die, alas! in those days, was the
supreme virtue of those who had never known vice.

Hoffmann reflected that, if he had come to Paris to
see extraordinary things, his journey was not a failure.

Somewhat comforted by the philosophy of history, he
said to himself, —

"There is still the theatre. Let us go to the theatre.
I am well aware that, after the actress I have just seen,
those who act in ordinary tragedy or opera will have no
effect on me, but I will be indulgent. One must not
ask too much of women who die of laughing only. But
I will try and remember that square so that I may never
go there again while I live."

IX.

THE JUDGMENT OF PARIS.

HOFFMANN was a man of sudden transitions. After Place de la Révolution and the tumultuous mob gathered about a scaffold, the gloomy sky and the blood, he must needs have the glare of many candles, the joyous multitude, flowers, in a word, life. He was not sure that he could by that means banish the memory of the sight he had just witnessed, but he was determined at all events to give his eyes a change of scene and to satisfy himself that there were still people in the world who lived and laughed.

He bent his steps toward the Opéra therefore; but he arrived there without knowing how he arrived. His resolution walked in front, and he followed it as a blind man follows his dog, while his mind travelled in an opposite direction, among sights and sounds of a very different nature.

As on Place de la Révolution, there was a crowd on the boulevard where the home of the Opera then was, on the present site of the Théâtre de la Porte Saint-Martin.

Hoffmann stopped on the outskirts of the crowd and looked at the poster.

They were playing the "Judgment of Paris," a ballet-pantomime in three acts, by Monsieur Gardel the younger, a son of Marie-Antoinette's dancing-master, and at a later period master of ballets to the emperor.

"The ' Judgment of Paris,' " muttered the poet, gazing fixedly at the poster, as if to engrave in his mind, with the aid of his eyes and ears, the meaning of those three words, the " Judgment of Paris."

But to no purpose did he repeat the syllables composing the title of the ballet. They seemed to him utterly devoid of meaning, so hard was it for his mind to cast out the terrible memories with which it was filled, to make room for the work borrowed by Monsieur Gardel the younger from Homer's " Iliad."

What a strange epoch was that when one could see a condemnation in the morning, an execution in the afternoon, and ballet-dancing in the evening, all in the same day, and when one ran the risk of being arrested one's self upon recovering from all that excitement !

Hoffmann realized that unless somebody else told him what the play was to be, he should never succeed in finding out, and that he might perhaps go mad before that poster.

So he walked up to a stout gentleman who was standing in the line with his wife, — for in all time stout men have had a mania for standing in line with their wives, — and said to him, —

" What do they play this evening, monsieur ? "

" You can see on the poster, monsieur," the stout man replied; " the ' Judgment of Paris.' "

" The Judgment of Paris," Hoffmann repeated. " Oh, yes, the Judgment of Paris; I know what that is."

The stout man looked at his strange questioner and shrugged his shoulders with a gesture expressive of the most profound contempt for this young man, who, in those ultra-mythological days, could have forgotten for an instant what the judgment of Paris was.

"Would you like an explanation of the ballet, citizen?" said a dealer in libretti, approaching Hoffmann.

"Yes, give me one!"

It was an additional proof to our hero that he was really going to the play, and he needed it.

He opened the book and glanced over its contents.

It was daintily printed on fine white paper and enriched by a preface by the author.

"What a marvellous thing man is!" thought Hoffmann, looking over the few lines of the preface, which he had not as yet read, but which he proposed to read; "and how he marches on alone, selfish and indifferent, along the pathway of his own interests and ambitions, while forming a part of the common mass of mankind! For instance, here is a man, this Monsieur Gardel the younger, who produced this ballet on March 5, 1793, that is to say, six weeks after the king's death, — six weeks after one of the most momentous events in the world's history; and on the day when this ballet was produced, he had private emotions of his own, distinct from the general emotion. His heart beat fast when his work was applauded; and if, at that moment, somebody had spoken to him of the event which still thrilled the world, and had mentioned King Louis XVI., he would have exclaimed: 'Louis XVI., who is he?' And then, as if, from the day when he put his ballet before the public, the whole world could have no other subject in its mind than that choregraphic event, he wrote a preface in explanation of his pantomime. Well, well! let us read his little preface. I will see if, dismissing from my mind the date when it was written, I find in it any trace of the circumstances amid which it first saw the light."

Hoffmann leaned upon the railing of the theatre, and this is what he read: —

"I have always noticed in ballet-pantomimes that scenic effects and varied and pleasing *divertissements* are what most attract the public and obtain the most enthusiastic applause."

"I must confess that that's a very interesting discovery," thought Hoffmann, unable to repress a smile at that first display of ingenuousness. "What! he really has noticed that the points that attract the public in ballets are scenic effects and varied and pleasing *divertissements!* How polite he is to Messieurs Haydn, Pleyel, and Méhul, who wrote the music for the 'Judgment of Paris!'" Let us see what else he says."

"In accordance with that observation, I sought a subject which could be so treated as to display the great talents in the matter of dancing which the Paris Opera alone possesses, and which would at the same time permit me to carry out such ideas as chance might suggest to me. Poetic history is the inexhaustible soil which the master of the ballet should cultivate. It is not without thorns; but one must know how to put them aside in order to pluck the rose."

"Well! upon my word! there's a sentence to be put in a golden frame!" cried Hoffmann. "Such things are written nowhere but in France."

He looked down at the book once more, intending to continue the perusal of those interesting aphorisms which were beginning to cheer him up a little; but his mind, momentarily diverted from its real preoccupation, gradually returned to it. The letters became confused under the dreamer's eyes. He let fall the hand that held the "Judgment of Paris," fixed his eyes on the ground and muttered, —

" Poor woman! "

The ghost of Madame du Barry again passed through his memory.

Thereupon he shook his head as if to banish from it the gloomy realities of the present, purchased his ticket, and entered the theatre.

The great hall was full, and resplendent with flowers, jewels, silks, and bare shoulders. A loud, incessant hum, — the hum of perfumed women, of trivial words, like the noise that thousands of flies would make in a paper box, and consisting principally of remarks that leave the same trace on the mind that a butterfly's wings leave on the finger of a child who catches it, and, two minutes later, not knowing what to do with it, throws up his hand and restores its liberty.

Hoffmann took a seat in the orchestra, and under the influence of the glowing atmosphere of the place, he succeeded in believing for a moment that he had been there since morning, and that the sorowful scene he had witnessed was a nightmare and not reality. Thereupon his memory, like every man's memory, which has two reflectors, one in the heart and the other in the mind, turned back insensibly, as a natural result of more cheerful impressions, toward the gentle maiden he had left behind him, whose portrait he could feel beating like another heart against his own heart. He looked at all the women who surrounded him, all those white shoulders, all those masses of light or dark hair, all those graceful arms, all those hands playing with the sticks of a fan or coquettishly arranging the flowers in a head-dress, and he smiled to himself as he uttered Antonia's name, as if that name were sufficient to banish any thought of comparison between her who bore it and all those other women, and to transport him to a world

of memories immeasurably more charming than all those
real forms, however beautiful they might be. Then,
as if that were not enough, as if he were afraid that the
portrait, which his mind conjured up across the space
that lay between them, might be effaced in the ideal
form in which it appeared to him, Hoffmann softly
slipped his hand into his breast, grasped the locket as a
timid girl grasps a bird in its nest, and, after making
sure that no one could see him and defile with a glance
the lovely image he held in his hand, he softly took
out the young girl's portrait, held it up before his eyes,
worshipped it for a moment with his glance, and, after
putting it devoutly to his lips, concealed it once more
over his heart. Nor could anybody divine the joy that
filled the heart of the young man with the black hair
and pale complexion as a result of what seemed to be
no more than the simple motion of putting his hand
into his waistcoat.

At that moment the signal was given, and the first
notes of the overture ran gayly through the orchestra,
like finches quarrelling in a thicket.

Hoffmann sat down and opened both ears to the
music, trying to become once more a man like those
about him, that is to say, an attentive spectator.

But after five minutes he ceased to listen, and no
longer cared to hear. That was not the sort of music to
fix Hoffmann's wandering attention, especially as he
heard it twice over, for a neighbor, who was doubtless
an habitué of the Opera and an admirer of Messrs.
Haydn, Pleyel, and Méhul, accompanied the melodies of
those gentlemen with perfect accuracy in a sort of falsetto
undertone. In addition to that accompaniment with his
mouth, he accompanied the music with his fingers, tapping his long tapering nails, in perfect time and with

fascinating dexterity, on the snuffbox he held in his hand.

Hoffmann, with the instinctive curiosity which is naturally the most prominent characteristic of all observing minds, examined with interest this personage who constituted himself, so to speak, a private orchestra grafted on the general orchestra.

In very truth he well deserved to be examined.

Imagine a small man wearing a black coat, waistcoat, and breeches, white shirt and cravat, of a whiteness that was more than white and almost as fatiguing to the eyes as the silvery reflection of snow. Cover half of this small man's hands, — thin hands, transparent as wax, which stood out against the black cloth as if they were lighted within, — cover them with ruffles of fine linen pleated with the greatest care and flexible as the leaves of the lily, and you will have an idea of the whole of the body. Now look at the head, and look at it as Hoffmann did, with curiosity mingled with amazement. Imagine a face oval in shape, the brow polished like ivory, sparse, yellow hair, growing here and there like clumps of bushes in a field. Suppress the eyebrows, and below the places where they should be, put two holes and in them a pair of eyes as cold as glass, almost always staring into vacancy, and the more easily believed to be inanimate, because you would look in vain therein for the luminous point which God placed in the eye as a spark on the hearth of life. Those blue eyes are like sapphires, neither gentle nor stern. They see, to be sure, but they do not look. A long, thin, pointed nose, a small mouth, with lips half-opened, showing teeth that are not white but of the same waxen shade as the skin, as if they had received a slight infiltration of pale blood and had retained a tinge of it, a pointed chin,

shaved with the greatest care, protruding cheek-bones, —
cheeks in which there are holes large enough to hold a
walnut, — such were the characteristic features of the
spectator who sat beside Hoffmann.

He might have been fifty years old or thirty. If he
had been eighty it would have been in no wise extraordinary. If he had been only twelve it would not
have seemed improbable. It seemed as if he must have
come into the world as he then was. He had certainly
never been any younger, and it was possible that he
might have looked older. It seemed as if, upon touching his skin, you would have had the same sensation of
cold as upon touching the skin of a serpent or a dead
body.

But he certainly loved music.

From time to time his lips parted a little more under
the impulse of sensuous enjoyment, and three little
folds, exactly alike on both sides, described a semi-
circle from the corners of his mouth and remained there
for five minutes, then gradually faded away like the
circles made by a stone falling into the water, which
spread out farther and farther until they are no longer
distinguishable on the surface.

Hoffmann did not weary of gazing at this man, who
felt that he was being examined, but gave no outward
indication of the feeling. He sat so perfectly still that
our poet, who had in his mind at that time the seed of
the fancy that was to give birth to " Coppelius," rested
his hands on the back of the seat in front, leaned forward, and turned his head to the right, trying to obtain
a full-face view of him whose profile only he had seen
thus far.

The little man looked at Hoffmann without surprise,
smiled upon him, nodded his head amicably, kept his

eyes fixed upon the same point, invisible to everybody but himself, and continued to accompany the orchestra.

"It's strange!" said Hoffmann, sitting back in his chair, "I would have bet that he wasn't alive."

And as if, although he had seen his neighbor move his head, he was not thoroughly convinced that the rest of his body was alive, he looked again at his hands. He was then struck by the fact that the snuffbox with which those hands were toying, an ebony snuffbox, was embellished with a small death's head in diamonds.

Everything seemed fated, on that day, to assume a fantastic shape in Hoffmann's eyes; but he was determined to gain his end, so he leaned forward as he had done before, and fixed his eyes upon the snuffbox at such close quarters that his lips almost touched the hand that held it.

The owner, seeing that his snuffbox was an object of such engrossing interest to his neighbor, silently passed it to him, so that he might examine it at his leisure.

Hoffmann took it, turned it over and over twenty times, and at last opened it.

There was snuff inside!

X.

ARSÈNE.

HAVING examined the snuffbox with the utmost attention, Hoffmann restored it to its owner, thanking him with a silent motion of the head to which the other replied with a motion as courteous, but, if such a thing were possible, even more silent.

"Now let us see if he will speak," said Hoffmann to himself; and he turned to his neighbor and said, —

"I beg you to pardon my presumption, monsieur, but that little death's head in diamonds on your snuffbox surprised me very much at first, for it 's an unusual ornament for that sort of thing."

"Indeed I believe it is the only one ever made," replied the stranger in a metallic voice, whose tones resembled the sound made by striking silver coins together. "It came into my hands from some grateful heirs, whose father I attended."

"You are a physician ? "

"Yes, monsieur."

"And did you cure the father of those young people ? "

"On the other hand, monsieur, we had the misfortune to lose him."

"I understand their gratitude."

The physician began to laugh.

His replies did not interrupt his humming, and he was still humming as he said, —

"Yes, I believe I killed that old man."

" How did you kill him ? "

" I tried a new remedy on him. *Mon Dieu!* in an hour he was dead. Really it's very amusing."

He continued to hum.

" You seem fond of music, monsieur ? " queried Hoffmann.

" Yes, monsieur; especially this."

" The devil ! " thought Hoffmann, " this fellow goes astray in music as well as in medicine."

At that moment the curtain rose.

The strange doctor took a pinch of snuff and settled himself as comfortably as possible in his stall, like a man who proposes to lose no part of the spectacle he is about to witness.

Meanwhile he said to Hoffmann, as if upon reflection, —

" You are a German, monsieur ? "

" I am."

" I recognized your nationality by your accent.' A fine country, but a wretched accent."

Hoffmann bowed in response to that half-complimentary, half-critical remark.

" You have come to France — what for ? "

" To see."

" And what have you seen thus far ? "

" I have seen a guillotining, monsieur."

" Were you on Place de la Révolution to-day ? "

" I was."

" Then you were a witness of Madame du Barry's death ? "

" Yes, " said Hoffmann with a sigh.

" I knew her well, " continued the doctor in a confidential tone, and so emphasizing the word *knew* as to impart to it its fullest signification. " She was a lovely girl, on my word ! "

" Did you attend her too ? "

"No, but I attended her negro boy, Zamore."

" The wretch! I was told that it was he who de-
nounced his mistress."

" The little negro was an ardent patriot, I tell you! "

" You would have done well to do with him as you
did with the old man, — you know, the old man of the
snuff box."

" What was the use ? he had no heirs."

And the doctor laughed again.

" Were you present at the execution yourself, monsieur ? " said Hoffmann, who felt an irresistible desire to
speak of the poor creature, whose bleeding image
haunted him.

" No. Had she grown thin ? "

" Who ? "

" The countess."

" I can't tell you, monsieur."

" Why not ? "

" Because I saw her for the first time on the tumbril."

" I am sorry for that. I would have liked to know,
for she was very plump when I knew her; but I will
go and see her body to-morrow. Ah! see, look at
that."

The doctor pointed to the stage where at that moment
Monsieur Vestris, who was playing the part of Paris,
appeared on Mount Ida and went through all sorts of
antics with the nymph Œnone.

Hoffmann glanced at what his neighbor pointed out to
him; but, after assuring himself that the sombre-faced
physician was really paying close attention to the pantomime, and that what he had heard and said had left no
trace on his mind, he said to himself, —

" It would be interesting to see this fellow weep."

"Do you know the subject of the play?" the doctor continued after a silence of a few moments.

"No, monsieur."

"It's very interesting. Indeed, there are some touching situations in it. A friend of mine and myself had tears in our eyes the other night."

"A friend of his!" muttered the poet; "what sort of a creature can a friend of this man's be? He must be a grave-digger."

"Ah! bravo! bravo! Vestris," shouted the little man, clapping his hands.

The physician had selected for this manifestation of his admiration the moment when Paris, as the book Hoffmann had purchased at the door informed him, seized his spear and flew to the succor of certain shepherds who were running in terror from a terrible lion.

I am not over-curious, but I would have liked to see the lion.

So ended the first act.

Thereupon the doctor stood up, turned about, leaned against the back of the stall in front of his, and, substituting a little opera-glass for his snuffbox, began to inspect the women in the audience.

Hoffmann mechanically followed the direction of the opera-glass and noticed with amazement that every person upon whom it rested instantly started and turned her eyes toward the man who was looking at her, exactly as if she were constrained to do it by some invisible force. And she would remain in that position until the doctor turned his glass away.

"Did that opera-glass come to you from anybody's heir, monsieur?" queried Hoffmann.

"No, it came from Monsieur de Voltaire."

"Did you know him too?"

"Well; we were very intimate."

"Were you his physician ? "

"He did not believe in medicine. To be sure, he did n't believe in much of anything."

"Is it true that he died while he was confessing ? "

"He, monsieur! Arouet! nonsense! not only did he not confess, but he gave the priest who came to attend him a warm welcome. I can tell you all about it, for I was there."

"What happened, pray ? "

'Arouet was dying. Tersac, his curé, appeared and said to him first of all, like a man who has no time to waste, 'Monsieur, do you believe in the trinity of Jesus Christ ? '

"' Leave me in peace, monsieur, I beg you,' replied Voltaire.

"' But, monsieur,' continued Tersac, ' it is important that I should know whether you recognize Jesus Christ as the son of God.'

"' In the devil's name ! ' cried Voltaire, ' don't mention that man to me again ! ' And summoning what little strength he still had, he struck the curé a blow in the face, and died. How I laughed ! *Mon Dieu !* how I laughed ! "

"It was laughable," said Hoffmann in a disdainful tone; "and that was just the way that the author of ' La Pucelle ' should die."

"Ah! yes, ' La Pucelle ! ' cried the man in black. "What a masterpiece, monsieur! What an admirable piece of work! I know but one book that can be compared with it."

"What is that ? "

"' Justine,' by Monsieur de Sade. "Do you know ' Justine ' ? "

"No, monsieur."

"And the Marquis de Sade?"

"No better."

"You see, monsieur" continued the doctor enthusiastically, "Justine is the most immoral book imaginable. It is Crebillon *fils* naked. It is wonderful. I attended a girl who read it."

"And did she die like your old man?"

"Yes, monsieur, but she died very happy."

And the doctor's eyes snapped at the reminiscence.

The signal was given for the second act. Hoffmann was not sorry, for his neighbor terrified him.

"Ah!" said the doctor, resuming his seat with a smile of satisfaction, "now we shall see Arsène."

"Who is Arsène?"

"Don't you know her?"

"No, monsieur."

"The devil! Don't you know anything at all, young man? Arsène is Arsène, that's the whole story. Besides you will soon see her."

And before the orchestra played a note the doctor began to hum the introduction to the second act.

The curtain rose.

The stage represented *a bower of flowers and greenery through which flowed a stream from a spring at the foot of a cliff.*

Hoffmann buried his face in his hands. Most assuredly, what he saw and heard was not powerful enough to divert his mind from the painful thoughts and ghastly memory that had led him thither.

"What difference would it have made," he thought, recurring suddenly to the impressions of the day, "what difference under heaven would it have made, if they had let that wretched woman live? What harm would it have done if that heart had continued to beat, that mouth to breathe? What misfortune would have happened? Why so suddenly put a stop to it all? By what right do they arrest life in its prime? She would be at home among all these women, whereas at this moment her poor body, the body that was beloved by a king, is lying in the mud of a cemetery, headless, without flowers, without a cross to mark her grave. My God, how she shrieked! how she shrieked! and then all of a sudden — "

Again he hid his face in his hands.

"What am I doing here?" he said to himself. "Ah! I will go away."

And perhaps he was really on the point of going away, when, as he raised his head, he saw on the stage a danseuse who did not appear in the first act, and whom the whole audience were watching as she danced, spellbound and breathless.

"Oh! how beautiful that woman is!" cried Hoffmann, loud enough for his neighbors and the danseuse herself to hear him.

The woman who had called forth that sudden admiration looked down at the young man who had involuntarily uttered the exclamation, and Hoffmann thought that she thanked him with a glance.

He blushed and started as if he had received an electric shock.

Arsène, for Arsène it was, — that is to say, the danseuse whose name the little old man had mentioned, — was really a beautiful creature, and her beauty had none of the characteristics of ordinary, traditional beauty.

She was tall, admirably built, and of a transparent pallor under the rouge with which her cheeks were covered. Her feet were very small, and when she

alighted on the stage you would have said that her toes
rested on a cloud, for there was not the slightest sound.
Her figure was so slight, so flexible, that no snake could
have twisted itself about as she did.   Every time that
she straightened herself up and leaned backward, you
would have thought that her corsets would burst, and
the vigor of her dancing and the assured poise of her
body enabled one to divine that she was perfectly well
aware of her flawless beauty, and that she possessed an
ardent nature which, like Messalina's of old, might
sometimes be fatigued but never surfeited.   She did not
smile as dancers commonly smile; her ruddy lips almost
never parted; not that they concealed ugly teeth, oh!
no, for when she bestowed a smile upon Hoffmann at
the moment when he so artlessly expressed his admiration aloud, our poet caught a glimpse of a double row
of pearls, so white and regular, that it seemed that she
must conceal them behind her lips so that the air should
not mar them.   In her hair, which was black and glossy,
with a bluish sheen, were entwined large acanthus
leaves and bunches of grapes, whose shadow played
upon her bare shoulders.   Her eyes were large and
clear and brilliant, so brilliant that they lighted up
everything about her, and if she had danced in the
darkness, she would have illumined the place where she
danced.   Another circumstance that added to the originality of her appearance was that, without any apparent
reason, she wore in her rôle of nymph, — for she was
acting or rather dancing a nymph, — she wore, we say,
a narrow black velvet necklace fastened by a clasp, or
at all events by an object which seemed to be of the
shape of a clasp, and which, being made of diamonds,
cast a dazzling gleam.

The doctor was gazing at the woman with all his eyes,

and his soul — such soul as he might have — seemed to hang upon her movements. It was very plain that, as long as she danced, he did not breathe.

Thereupon Hoffmann noticed a curious fact. Whether she moved to right or left, backward or forward, Arsène's eyes never swerved from the line of the doctor's eyes, and there was a visible correlation between their glances. Furthermore Hoffmann distinctly saw the rays cast by the clasp of Arsène's neckband and those cast by the doctor's death's head meet half-way between them, collide and rebound, myriads of white, red, and golden sparks following the collision.

" Will you lend me your opera-glass, monsieur ? " said Hoffmann, breathing hard and not turning his head, for it was impossible for him, too, to take his eyes from Arsène.

The doctor put out his hand toward Hoffmann without making the slightest movement of the head, so that their hands sought each other for some moments in space before they met.

Hoffmann seized the opera-glass at last and glued his eyes to it.

" It is strange," he muttered.

" What is strange ? " demanded the doctor.

" Nothing, nothing," replied Hoffmann, who desired to give his whole attention to what he saw. In truth, what he saw was strange.

The opera-glass brought everything so close to his eyes that Hoffmann put out his hand two or three times, thinking that he could grasp Arsène, who no longer seemed to be at the end of the glass in which her image was reflected, but directly between the two barrels of the glass. Thus our German lost no detail of the dancer's beauty, and her glances, so penetrating even at

a distance, surrounded his brow with a circle of flame
and made the blood boil in the veins at his temples.
His heart made a terrible uproar in his breast.

"Who is that woman?" he asked in a faint voice,
without taking the glass from his eyes, and without
moving a muscle.

"It is Arsène, as I told you before," replied the
doctor, whose lips alone seemed alive, and whose staring
eyes were riveted on the dancer.

"She has a lover, of course?"

"Yes."

"Whom she loves?"

"So they say."

"Is he rich?"

"Very rich."

"Who is he?"

"Look at the lower proscenium box at your left."

"I can't turn my head."

"Make an effort."

Hoffmann made an effort, so painful that it extorted
a cry from him, as if the chords in his neck had turned
to marble and had broken at that moment.

He looked at the box mentioned by the doctor. In
it there was but one man, but that man, crouching like
a lion upon the velvet rail, seemed to fill it completely.

He was a man of thirty-two or thirty-three years,
with a face seamed by passion. One would have said
that a volcanic eruption rather than the smallpox had
hollowed out the deep valley that crossed and recrossed
on that upheaved flesh. His eyes were naturally small,
but they were opened to an unnatural extent by internal
convulsions. Sometimes they were empty and lifeless
as an extinct crater; sometimes they shot flames like a
crater in full eruption. He did not applaud by clap-

ping his hands, but by striking the railing, and he
seemed to shake the building with every blow.

"Great heaven!" said Hoffmann, "is that a man?"

"Yes, yes, it's a man," replied the little man in
black. "Yes, it's a man and a good deal of a man
too."

"What's his name?"

"Don't you know him?"

"Why, no, I arrived only yesterday."

"Well, that is Danton."

"Danton!" exclaimed Hoffmann with a sudden start.
"Oho! and he is Arsène's lover?"

"He is her lover."

"And he loves her, of course?"

"Madly. He is jealous to ferocity."

But, interesting as the sight of Danton was, Hoffmann
had already turned his eyes back to Arsène, whose
silent dance was a weird thing to see.

"One more question, monsieur."

"Say on."

"What is the shape of the clasp that holds her
necklace?"

"It is a guillotine."

"A guillotine!"

"Yes. They make lovely ones now, and all our
fashionable women wear at least one. Danton gave
Arsène the one she wears."

"A guillotine, a guillotine at the neck of a ballet-
dancer!" repeated Hoffmann, who felt that his brain
was in a whirl. "A guillotine, why?"

And our German, who might well have been taken
for a madman, stretched out his arms before him as if to
seize something; for, by a strange optical delusion, the
distance between Arsène and himself steadily diminished,

and it seemed to him that he could hear the hot breathing of that chest, whose bosoms, half uncovered, rose and fell as if under the embrace of pleasure. Hoffmann was in that state of excitement in which one feels as if he were breathing fire, and fears lest his emotions rend his body.

"Enough! enough!" he said.

But the dance continued, and the hallucination was so complete that Hoffmann's mind, dwelling upon the two strongest impressions of the day, confused the stage before him with Place de la Révolution, and sometimes he fancied that he saw Madame du Barry's headless body dancing in Arsène's place, and sometimes that Arsène came dancing to the foot of the guillotine and into the executioner's hands.

In the young man's excited imagination there was a medley of flowers and blood, of dancing and the death-agony, of life and death.

But over and above it all was the magnetic attraction that drew him toward the young woman. Every time that those two slender legs passed before his eyes, every time that those filmy skirts rose a little higher, a shudder ran through his whole frame, his lips became dry, his breath parched and hot, and desire seized upon him as it seizes upon a man of twenty.

In that condition of affairs Hoffmann had but one refuge, — Antonia's portrait, the locket that he wore upon his heart; to confront this sensual love with a pure and holy love, to appeal to chaste memories in face of this potent reality.

He seized the portrait and put it to his lips; but he had no sooner made the movement than he heard the shrill, sneering laugh of his neighbor who was looking at him with a mocking air.

"Let me go out," he cried. "Let me go out. I can remain here no longer!"

Like a madman he left the orchestra, treading on the feet and brushing against the legs of the tranquil spectators, who cursed and swore at the idiot who had the strange whim of going out in the middle of a ballet.

XI.

THE SECOND PERFORMANCE OF THE JUDGMENT OF PARIS.

But Hoffmann's impulse did not carry him very far. He stopped at the corner of Rue Saint-Martin.

He was gasping for breath; his forehead was bathed in perspiration.

He passed his left hand across his forehead, placed his right hand on his breast, and drew a long breath.

At that moment some one touched his shoulder. He jumped.

"*Pardieu!* it is himself!" said a voice.

He turned and uttered an exclamation.

It was his friend Zacharias Werner.

The two young men threw themselves into each other's arms.

Then these two questions crossed each other: —

"What are you doing here?"

"Where are you going?"

"I arrived yesterday," said Hoffmann. "I saw Madame du Barry guillotined, and I came to the Opéra for distraction."

"I arrived six months ago. For the last five months I have seen twenty to twenty-five persons guillotined every day, and I am going to play cards for distraction."

"Aha!"

"Will you come with me?"

"No, thanks."

" You are making a mistake, for I am in a lucky vein. With your usual good luck, you would make your fortune. You must have been horribly bored at the Opéra, accustomed as you are to real music. Come with me, and I 'll take you where you can hear some."

" Music ? "

" Yes, the music of gold; and, in addition to that, all forms of pleasure are combined where I am going: charming women, a delicious supper, and terrific gambling! "

" Thanks, my friend, it 's impossible! I have promised; more than that, I have sworn."

" To whom ? "

" Antonia."

" So you have seen her ? "

" I love her, my friend, I adore her."

" Ah! I understand, that is what delayed you so; and you swore to her ? "

" I swore to her not to gamble, and — "

Hoffmann hesitated.

" And what else ? "

" And to remain true to her," he faltered.

" Then you must n't come to 113."

" What is 113 ? "

" It 's the house I mentioned just now. I have n't taken any oath myself, so I am off. Farewell, Theodor."

" Farewell, Zacharias."

And Werner hurried away while Hoffmann remained nailed to his place.

When Werner was a hundred yards away Hoffmann remembered that he had forgotten to ask his address, and that the only address he had given him was that of the gambling-house.

But that address was written in Hoffmann's mind as it was over the door of the fatal house itself, in letters of flame !

Meanwhile what had taken place had allayed Hoffmann's remorse to some extent. Human nature is thus constituted, always indulgent to itself, inasmuch as its indulgence is pure selfishness.

He had sacrificed the thirst for gambling to Antonia, and he thought that he had kept his oath, forgetting that it was because he was all ready to break the most important part of that oath, that he was standing at the corner of the boulevard and Rue Saint-Martin as if he were nailed there.

But, as I have said, his resistance in the case of Werner had made him indulgent in the matter of Arsène. He determined, therefore, to adopt a middle course, and, instead of returning to the theatre, — a step to which the demon of temptation urged him with all his strength, — to wait at the stage door and see her come out.

Hoffmann was too well acquainted with the topography of theatres not to find the stage door very soon. He discovered, on Rue de Bondy, a long passage-way very dimly lighted, damp and dirty, through which men in shabby garments passed like ghosts, and he knew at once that that was the door which gave ingress and egress to the poor creatures whom red and white and blue paint, gauze and silk and spangles, transformed into gods and goddesses.

The moments passed. Snow was falling, but Hoffmann was so excited by the strange apparition he had witnessed, in which there was a touch of the supernatural, that he did not feel the sensation of cold that seemed to afflict the passers-by. Vainly did he condense in

vapor that was almost tangible the breath that issued
from his mouth. His hands were none the less burning
hot and his brow moist with perspiration. Leaning
against the wall, with his eyes riveted on the corri-
dor, he stood perfectly motionless, so that the snow,
which continued to fall more heavily, slowly covered
him as with a shroud, and gradually transformed the
student in his German cap and overcoat into a marble
statue.

At last those who were first at liberty to depart began
to emerge from the narrow passage, then the machinists,
then all the nameless crew who live upon the theatre,
then the male artists, who require less time for dressing
than the women, then the women, and at last the fair
danseuse, whom Hoffmann recognized not by her lovely
face alone, but by that undulatory motion of the hips
which was peculiar to her, and by the narrow velvet
ribbon at her neck, upon which sparkled the strange
jewel made fashionable by the Terror.

The instant that Arsène appeared in the doorway, and
before Hoffmann had time to stir, a carriage drove up
rapidly, the door was thrown open, and the girl jumped
in as lightly as if she were still pirouetting on the
stage. A form appeared through the window, and
Hoffmann thought that he recognized the man of the
proscenium box; that form received the beautiful nymph
in its arms; then, without a word of direction to the
coachman, the carriage drove away at a gallop.

All this that we have described in eighteen or twenty
lines took place as rapidly as the lightning flashes.

Hoffmann uttered a sort of shriek as he saw the carriage drive away, stepped out from the wall like a statue
leaving its niche, and shaking off the snow with which
he was covered, darted in pursuit of the carriage.

But it was drawn by two powerful horses of such speed that it was impossible for the young man, however swift his reckless pace, to overtake them.

So long as the carriage followed the boulevard, all went well. So long as it followed Rue de Bourbon-Villeneuve, recently re-christened Rue Neuve-Égalité, all went well; but when it reached Place des Victoires, otherwise Place de la Victoire Nationale, it turned to the right and vanished from Hoffmann's sight.

Being no longer sustained by the sound of the wheels or the sight of the carriage, the young man's strength failed him. He stopped for a moment at the corner of Rue Neuve-Eustache, and leaned against the wall to recover his breath. Then, seeing and hearing nothing, he looked about, judging that it was time for him to return to his lodgings.

It was no simple matter for Hoffmann to extricate himself from the labyrinth of streets that form an almost inextricable network from Pointe Saint-Eustache to Quai de la Ferraille. However, thanks to the numerous patrols circulating through the streets, thanks to his satisfactory passport, and thanks to the ready proof afforded by the date of the visa at the barrier that he had arrived only the night before, he obtained from the citizen militia such precise directions that he succeeded in finding his hotel and his little room, where he locked himself in, alone to all appearance, but, in reality, accompanied by a vivid memory of what had taken place.

From that moment Hoffmann was haunted by two visions, one of which gradually faded away, while the other gradually became more and more vivid.

The vision that faded away was the pale, distorted face of La du Barry, as she was dragged from the

Conciergerie to the tumbril and from the tumbril to the scaffold.

The vision that assumed more and more reality was the bright and smiling countenance of the lovely dancer, as she skipped from the back of the stage to the foot-lights and whirled from the footlights to one side after the other.

Hoffmann did his utmost to banish that vision. He took his brushes from his box and painted. He took his violin from its case and played. He asked for pen and ink and wrote poetry. But the poetry that he wrote was in praise of Arsène. The air that he played was the air to which she appeared, and whose buoyant notes seemed to lift her as if they had had wings; and the sketches he made were portraits of her, with the same velvet necklace, the curious ornament fastened about Arsène's neck by such a curious clasp.

During all that night, during all the next day, during all the following night and day, Hoffmann saw but one thing or rather two things: on one side the bizarre danseuse, and on the other side the no less bizarre doctor. There was such a close affinity between the two that Hoffmann could not think of one without the other. And so, during that period of hallucination, in which he saw Arsène always dancing about the stage, it was not the music of the orchestra that rang in his ears, but the doctor's soft humming and the gentle tapping of his fingers on the ebony snuffbox; and then, from time to time, a flash passed before his eyes, blind-ing him with showers of sparks. It was the double gleam cast by the doctor's snuffbox and the dancer's clasp. It was the sympathetic attraction between the diamond guillotine and the diamond skull. It was the fixed stare of the doctor's eyes, which seemed at his

will to attract and repel the fascinating danseuse, as the
serpent's eye attracts and repels the bird it fascinates.

Twenty times, a hundred times, a thousand times, the
idea of going again to the Opéra came to Hoffmann's
mind; but, until the time came, he promised himself
that he would not yield to the temptation. Moreover,
he had combated the temptation in every way, having
recourse to his locket first, and then trying to write to
Antonia; but Antonia's portrait seemed to have taken
on such a sad expression that Hoffmann closed the locket
almost as soon as he opened it, and the first lines of
every letter he began were so labored and embarrassed
that he had torn up ten letters before he had written a
third of the first page.

At last the second day passed. At last the time for
opening the theatre approached. At last the clock
struck seven, and, at that last summons, Hoffmann,
as if carried away by a power stronger than himself,
rushed down the stairs and darted away in the direction
of Rue Saint-Martin.

That time, in less than quarter of an hour, without
asking any one to point out the way, he arrived at the
door of the Opéra as if an invisible guide had gone
before him.

But, strange to say, the door was not surrounded by
an eager crowd as it was two days before, either because
some incident unknown to Hoffmann had rendered the
performance less attractive, or because the audience
was already inside.

Hoffmann tossed his six francs to the ticket-seller,
received his ticket, and hurried into the hall.

The aspect of the place was greatly changed. In the
first place it was only half full; and then, in place of
the beautiful women and men of fashion he had expected

to see, he saw only women in short gowns and men in short jackets; no jewels, no flowers, no bare breasts rising and falling in the voluptuous atmosphere that reigns in aristocratic theatres; round caps and red caps, all adorned with huge national cockades; garments of dark hue, and a cloud of sadness on every face; and on either side a hideous, grinning bust, one laughter, the other sorrow, — the busts of Voltaire and Marat.

And lastly, the proscenium box at the left was only a dimly-lighted hole, a dark and untenanted aperture, — the cavern still, but without the lion.

There were two vacant seats, side by side, in the orchestra stalls. Hoffmann took one of them, the same he had occupied before. The other was the one the doctor had occupied, but, as we have said, it was vacant.

The first act was played through without Hoffmann's bestowing a thought upon the orchestra or the performers. He was familiar with the orchestra and had formed his opinion of it at a first hearing. The actors he cared but little about. He had not come to see them; he had come to see Arsène.

The curtain rose for the second act and the ballet began.

The young man's heart and soul and mind were all in suspense.

He was awaiting Arsène's appearance.

Suddenly he uttered an exclamation.

Arsène no longer took the part of Flore.

The woman who appeared in the part was a stranger to him, a woman like all other women.

All the fibres of that throbbing body relaxed. Hoffmann sank back in his chair with a long sigh and looked about him.

The little man in black was in his seat; but he no longer wore his diamond buckles, his diamond rings, nor carried his snuffbox with the skull in diamonds.

His buckles were of copper, his rings of silver gilt, his snuffbox of unpolished silver.

He no longer hummed; he no longer beat time.

How had he come there? Hoffmann had no idea. He had neither seen him come nor felt him pass.

" O monsieur ! " he cried.

" Say, citizen, my young friend, and call me thee and thou, if possible," said the little man in black, " or you will get my head cut off and your own too."

" In God's name where is she ? " asked Hoffmann.

" Ah, that 's the question. Where is she ? It seems that her tiger, who never takes his eyes off her, noticed day before yesterday that she exchanged signs with a young man in the orchestra stalls. It seems that that young man ran after the carriage; so that yesterday he forced Arsène to break her engagement, and she is no longer at the theatre."

" But how did the manager allow it ? "

" My young friend, the manager is anxious to keep his head on his shoulders, although it 's an ugly sort of head; but he says that he is used to it, and that another handsomer one might not graft readily."

" Ah ! mein Gott ! that 's why the place is so gloomy ! " cried Hoffmann. " That is why there are no flowers, no diamonds, no jewels ! That is why you have n't your diamond buckles, your diamond rings, and your diamond snuffbox ! That is why those two horrible busts are placed at the sides of the stage, instead of the busts of Apollo and Terpsichore ! Pah ! "

" Hoity-toity ! what 's that you say ? " exclaimed the

doctor. " Where did you see such a hall as you describe ? Where did you see me with diamond rings and diamond snuffboxes ? Where did you see the busts of Apollo and Terpsichore ? Why, it 's two years now since flowers ceased to bloom, since all the diamonds were turned into assignats, and the jewels melted down on the altar of the country.   As for myself, thank God ! I have never had any buckles but these copper ones, any other rings than this paltry silver gilt affair, any other snuffbox than this poor silver one.   As for the busts of Apollo and Terpsichore, they used to stand there once, but the friends of humanity broke the bust of Apollo and replaced it by the apostle Voltaire's, and the friends of the people shattered the bust of Terpsichore and replaced it by that of the god Marat."

" Oh ! " cried Hoffmann, " it is impossible.   I tell you that, day before yesterday, I saw this hall perfumed with flowers, resplendent with rich costumes, gleaming with diamonds, and men of fashion in the places occupied by yonder fishwomen in short gowns and yonder blackguards in *carmagnoles*.   I tell you that you had diamond buckles to your shoes, diamond rings on your fingers, a death's head in diamonds on your snuffbox. I tell you — "

" And I tell you, young man," rejoined the little man in black, " that day before yesterday *she* was here.   I tell you that her presence illumined everything.   I tell you that her breath made the roses bloom, made the jewels glisten, made your imaginary diamonds sparkle. I tell you that you love her, young man, and that you saw the hall through the prism of your love.   Arsène is no longer here; your heart is dead; your eyes are disenchanted.   You see swanskin. cotton. coarse cloth.

red caps, dirty hands, and dishevelled hair. In short you see the world as it is, things as they are."

"O my God!" cried Hoffmann, letting his head fall forward in his hands, "is all this true, and am I really so near going mad?"

XII.

THE WINE-SHOP.

HOFFMANN did not emerge from his lethargy until he felt a hand upon his shoulder.

He raised his head. All the lights were out, and everything was dark around him. The unlighted theatre seemed to him like the corpse of the theatre he had seen in full life. The soldier on guard alone was walking about, silent as the death watch; no lights, no orchestra, no brilliancy, no sound, save a single voice that mumbled in his ear, —

"Come, citizen, citizen, what are you doing here? You 're at the Opéra, citizen. People go to sleep here, to be sure, but not to bed."

Hoffmann finally looked in the direction from which the voice came, and saw a little old woman who was pulling him by his coat-collar.

It was the keeper of the orchestra stalls, who, being ignorant of the persistent spectator's intentions, did not wish to retire until she had seen him go out.

Once wakened from his torpor, however, Hoffmann made no resistance. He gave a sigh and rose, murmuring the word, —

"Arsène!"

"Oh! yes, Arsène," said the little old woman, "Arsène! So you are in love with her like everybody else, young man? It 's a great loss to the Opéra, especially to us box-openers."

"To you box-openers," said Hoffmann, overjoyed to find some one who would talk with him about the dancer. "How is it a loss to you that Arsène is no longer at the theatre?"

"*Dame!* that's easily explained. In the first place, whenever she danced she filled the house, and then there was a big demand for stools and chairs and little benches, —at the Opéra you have to pay for everything. People paid extra for the stools and chairs and little benches, and those were our small profits. I say small profits," added the old woman slyly, "because there were large profits beside, citizen, you understand."

"Large profits?"

"Yes."

And the old woman winked.

"What were the large profits? tell me, my good woman."

"The large profits came from those who asked questions about her, wanted to know her address, and sent notes to her. There's a price for everything, you understand; so much for answering questions, so much for the address, so much for the note. We did quite a little business, in fact, and earned an honest living."

The old woman heaved a sigh which might be compared, not unfavorably, to the one emitted by Hoffmann at the beginning of the dialogue we have reported.

"Aha!" said Hoffmann, "so you used to answer questions about her, to tell her address, and deliver notes to her, did you? Do you still do it?"

"Alas! monsieur, any information I could give you would be useless to you now. No one knows Arsène's address, and any note you might give me for her would be wasted. If you want any other, Madame Vestris, Mademoiselle Bigottini, Mademoiselle —"

"Thanks, my good woman, thanks. I don't care to know anything about anybody except Mademoiselle Arsène. Take this," said Hoffmann, taking three francs from his pocket, "for your trouble in waking me."

He left the old woman and walked slowly out to the boulevard, intending to follow the same road he had followed two nights before, the instinct that had guided him thither early in the evening having deserted him.

His feelings, however, were very different, and his gait bore witness to the difference in his feelings.

On the other occasion, his gait was that of a man who has seen Hope pass by, and who runs after her, not pausing to reflect that God has given her her long azure wings so that man may never overtake her. His mouth was open, and his breath came in gasps; his head was erect, and his arms outstretched. Now, on the contrary, he walked slowly, like the man who, after a vain pursuit of Hope, has lost sight of her; his mouth was tightly closed, his head bent, his arms hanging by his sides. The other time it had taken him hardly five minutes to go from Porte Saint-Martin to Rue Montmartre; this time it took him more than an hour, and still another hour to go from Rue Montmartre to his hotel; for in the state of dejection into which he had fallen, it mattered little to him whether he returned home early or late or not at all.

It is said that there is a special Providence for drunkards and lovers; that Providence, doubtless, watched over Hoffmann. It helped him to avoid the patrols; it helped him to find the quays, then the bridges, and then his hotel, where he appeared, to the great scandal of his landlady, at half-past one in the morning.

Meanwhile, through all his dejection, one little golden ray danced about in Hoffmann's imagination like a firefly in the darkness. The doctor,—assuming that the doctor really existed, and was not a mere creature of his imagination, a delusion of his mind,— the doctor had told him that Arsène had been taken away from the theatre by her lover, because that lover was jealous of a young man in the orchestra stalls, with whom Arsène had exchanged a too tender glance.

The doctor had also said that the thing that had stirred the tyrant's jealousy to its highest pitch was that that same young man had lain in ambush at the stage door, and had run like a madman behind the carriage. Now, the young man in the orchestra stalls who had exchanged passionate glances with Arsène was himself, Hoffmann; the young man who had lain in ambush at the stage door was himself; and, lastly, the young man who had run desperately behind the carriage, that young man likewise was himself, Hoffmann. Arsène must have noticed him, therefore, as she was paying the penalty of her momentary distraction; therefore, Arsène was suffering for him. He had entered the lovely dancer's life through the door of suffering; but he had entered it, that was the main point; it was for him to maintain his footing there. But how, by what means, through what channel could he correspond with Arsène, tell her who and what he was, and that he loved her? It would have been no small task for a full-blooded Parisian to find the fair Arsène in the wilderness of that immense city. It was an impossible task for Hoffmann, who had been there only three days and had great difficulty in finding himself.

And so Hoffmann did not even take the trouble to look for her; he felt that chance alone could help him. Every second day he looked at the advertisements of the Opéra, and every second day he was grieved to see that Paris was to deliver his judgment in the absence of one who was much more worthy of the apple than Venus.

At other times he did not think of going to the Opéra.

For an instant he had an idea of going to the Convention, or to the Cordeliers, to dog Danton's footsteps, and by watching him day and night to guess where he had hidden the lovely dancer.

He actually went to the Convention and to the Cordeliers, but Danton was not at either place; for seven or eight days he had not been seen at either. Weary of the battle he had fought for two years past, vanquished by ennui rather than by the superiority of his foes, Danton seemed to have withdrawn from the political arena.

Danton was said to be at his country estate. Where was his country estate? No one knew; some said at Reuil, others at Auteuil.

Danton was as hard to find as Arsène.

One would think perhaps that Arsène's absence would have led Hoffmann's thoughts back to Antonia; but, strange to say, it did nothing of the sort. In vain did Hoffmann put forth every effort to bring his mind back to the poor child: for an instant, by the force of his will, all the powers of his memory would be concentrated upon Master Gottlieb's studio; but, at the end of that instant, the scores heaped upon tables and pianos, Master Gottlieb stamping at his desk, Antonia lying on her couch, all disappeared, to give place to a huge, brilliantly-lighted frame, in which, at first, shadows moved to and fro; then those shadows became bodies, the bodies assumed mythological forms, and finally all those mythological forms, all those heroes, nymphs, gods, and demigods disappeared, to be succeeded by a single goddess, the goddess of gardens, the enchanting Flore, that is to say, the divine Arsène, the woman with the velvet necklace and diamond clasp. Thereupon Hoffmann would fall, not into a reverie but into a trance from which he could rouse himself only by plunging into real life, by elbowing the passers-by in the street, by rushing about in the crowd and the uproar.

And so when this hallucination that preyed upon Hoffmann became too vivid, he would go out, walk along the quay, cross Pont-Neuf, and never pause until he reached the corner of Rue de la Monnaie. There he had found a wine-shop which was the rendezvous of the hardest smokers in the capital. There Hoffmann could fancy himself in some English tavern, in some Dutch music-hall, or some German beer-garden, for the pipe-smoke made the atmosphere so thick that none but a smoker of the first rank could breathe it.

Once inside the *Fraternité*, Hoffmann would seat himself at a small table in the darkest corner, call for a bottle of beer from the brewery of Citizen Santerre, — who had recently resigned his commission as general of the Paris National Guard in favor of Citizen Henriot, — load to the brim the huge pipe with which we are already acquainted, and envelop himself within a few moments in a cloud of smoke as dense as that in which lovely Venus enveloped her son Æneas whenever that loving mother deemed it expedient to rescue her beloved child from the wrath of his enemies.

Eight or ten days had passed since Hoffmann's adventure at the Opéra and the disappearance of the beautiful danseuse; it was one o'clock in the afternoon. Hoffmann had been sitting in his wine-shop about half an hour, doing his best, with all the strength of his lungs, to surround himself with the circle of dense smoke which separated him from his neighbors, when it seemed to him that he distinguished something like a human figure through the vapor; that he heard, above all the noises of the place, the humming and tapping of the little man in black; furthermore, it seemed to him that, in the midst of the smoke, there was a luminous point from which sparks were flying. He opened his eyes, which were half-closed in a pleasant drowsiness, raised the lids with difficulty, and saw, upon a stool facing him, his neighbor at the Opéra; and he recognized him the more readily because the eccentric doctor had, or seemed to have, his diamond buckles on his shoes, his diamond rings on his fingers, and the snuffbox with the death's head.

"The devil!" said Hoffmann, "I am going mad again."

And he promptly closed his eyes.

But the more tightly his eyes were closed, the more distinctly Hoffmann heard the low humming accompaniment and the drumming with the fingers; and it was so distinct that Hoffmann realized that there must be a foundation of reality for it all, and that the only question was how much was real.

He opened one eye, then the other; the little man in black was still in the same place.

"Good morning, young man," he said to Hoffmann. "You were asleep, I think; take a pinch, it will rouse you."

He opened his snuffbox and offered it to the young man, who mechanically put out his hand, took a pinch of the snuff and inhaled it.

On the instant it seemed to him as if a bright light streamed into his mind.

"Ah! is it you, dear doctor?" he cried; "how glad I am to see you!"

"If you are so glad to see me," rejoined the doctor, "why haven't you looked for me?"

"As if I knew your address."

"Oh, that's a trifling difficulty. They would have given it to you at the nearest cemetery."

"But I don't know your name."

"The doctor with the death's head; everybody knows me by that name. Then there is one place where you are sure of finding me."

"Where is that?"

"At the Opéra. I am physician to the Opéra. You know that, for you have seen me there twice."

"Oh! the Opéra," said Hoffmann with a sigh, and a shake of the head.

"Yes; don't you go any more?"

"No, I don't go any more."

"Since Arsène ceased to take the part of Flore?"

"You have said it; and so long as she stays away, I shall not go."

"You love her, young man, you love her."

"I am not certain whether the disease I am suffering with is called love, but I do know that, if I don't see her again, I shall die of not seeing her, or go mad."

"*Peste!* you must n't go mad! you must n't die! There are few remedies for madness and none at all for death."

"What must I do then?"

"*Dame!* you must see her again."

"What do you say — see her again?"

"To be sure!"

"Do you know any way?"

"Perhaps."

"What is it?"

"Wait a moment."

And the doctor seemed lost in thought, winking his eyes and drumming on his snuffbox.

After a moment he opened his eyes and said, holding his fingers in the air over the box, —

"You are a painter, you told me?"

" Yes, painter, musician, and poet."

" We need only painting for the moment."

" Very good ! "

" Arsène has told me to find a painter for her."

" What to do ? "

" Why do people generally want painters ? *pardieu !* to paint her portrait."

" Arsène's portrait ! " cried Hoffmann, springing to his feet; " oh! I am ready! I am ready ! "

" Hush! remember that I am a serious-minded man."

" You are my preserver ! " cried Hoffmann, throwing his arms around the little man's neck.

" Youth, youth ! " muttered the latter, accompanying the word with the same sneering laugh that his death's head would have laughed, if it had been of life-size.

" Come! come ! " said Hoffmann.

" But you must have a box of colors, brushes, canvas."

" I have all those at home ; come ! "

" Very good," said the doctor.

And they left the wine-shop together.

XIII.

THE PORTRAIT.

As they left the wine-shop Hoffmann made a gesture to call a cab; but the doctor struck his thin hands together, and at that sound, which resembled the sound that a skeleton's hands would have made, a carriage lined with black, drawn by two black horses, and driven by a coachman dressed in black, drove up. Where was it standing? Where did it come from? It would have been as difficult for Hoffmann to say, as it would have been for Cinderella to say where the chariot came from in which she drove to Prince Miriflore's ball.

A little groom, with a black skin as well as black clothes, opened the door. Hoffmann and the doctor entered, seated themselves side by side, and the carriage at once rolled noiselessly away toward Hoffmann's lodgings.

When they reached the door Hoffmann hesitated about going up to his room. He was afraid that, as soon as his back was turned, carriage, horses, doctor, and servants would disappear as they had appeared. But for what purpose could doctor, carriage, horses, and servants have gone out of their way to take him, Hoffmann, from Rue de la Monnaie to Quai aux Fleurs? None at all.

Reassured by that simple application of the principles of logic, Hoffmann alighted from the carriage, entered the house, ran hastily upstairs, rushed into his room, seized his palette, brushes, and box of colors, selected the largest of his canvases, and descended as rapidly as he had ascended.

The carriage was still at the door.

Brushes, palette, and box of colors were bestowed inside the carriage. The canvas was intrusted to the groom.

Then the carriage rolled away as swiftly and silently as before.

Ten minutes later it stopped in front of a delightful little house on Rue de Hanovre, number 15.

Hoffmann made a note of the street and number, so that, in case of need, he might be able to return thither without the doctor's help.

The door opened. The doctor evidently was known, for the concierge did not even ask him where he was going. Hoffmann, with his brushes, his box of colors, his palette, and his canvas, followed the doctor and entered the house.

They went up to the first floor and entered a reception-room which might have been taken for the vestibule of the poet's house at Pompeii.

The reader will remember that the Greek style was fashionable at this time. Arsène's reception-room was frescoed and decorated with bronze candelabra and statues.

From the reception-room Hoffmann and the doctor entered the salon.

The salon was Greek like the reception-room, hung with Sedan cloth at seventy francs the ell. The carpet alone cost six thousand francs. The doctor called Hoffmann's attention to the carpet, which represented the battle of Arbela, copied from the famous mosaic at Pompeii.

Hoffmann, dazzled by such unheard-of magnificence, could not understand that such carpets were made to walk upon.

From the salon they entered the boudoir, which was hung with cashmere. At the end of the room was a low bed, also used as a couch, like that upon which Monsieur Guérin afterwards painted Dido listening to the adventures of Æneas. There Arsène had given orders for them to wait.

"Now, young man," said the doctor, "here you are in the house, and it is for you to conduct yourself in a becoming manner. It goes without saying that if the titular lover should surprise you here you would be a dead man."

"Oh!" cried Hoffmann, "let me see her again, just let me see her again, and — "

The words died upon his lips. He stood with staring eyes, arms extended, and heaving breast.

A door concealed in the wainscoting had opened, and Arsène appeared from behind a revolving mirror, a veritable divinity of the temple in which she deigned to appear to her adorer.

Her costume was the costume of Aspasia in all its olden magnificence, with her pearls in her hair, her gold-embroidered, purple cloak, her long white dress, caught in at the waist by a simple girdle of pearls, rings on her feet and hands, and, with it all, that strange ornament which seemed inseparable from her person, the velvet necklace, hardly four lines in width, and fastened by its lugubrious diamond-clasp.

"Ah! citizen, are you the one who is to paint my portrait?"

"Yes," stammered Hoffmann. "Yes, madame, and the doctor has kindly consented to be my sponsor."

He looked about as if to call upon the doctor to support his statement, but the doctor had disappeared.

"What!" he cried, sadly embarrassed.

"What are you looking for? What do you want, citizen?"

"Why, madame, I am looking for, I want — I want the doctor, the person who brought me here."

"What do you need of him," said Arsène, "so long as you are here?"

"But the doctor, the doctor?" said Hoffmann.

"Nonsense!" exclaimed Arsène, testily, "do you propose to waste time looking for him? The doctor is attending to his business; let us attend to ours."

"I am at your service, madame," said Hoffmann, trembling from head to foot.

"So you agree to paint my portrait?"

"I am the most fortunate man in the world to have been selected for such an honor; but I have only one fear."

"Bah! you are going to play the modest man. If you don't succeed I shall try somebody else. *He* is determined to have a portrait of me. I saw that you looked at me like a man who was likely to keep my face in his mind, and I gave you the preference."

"Thanks, thanks a hundred times!" cried Hoffmann, devouring Arsène with his eyes. "Oh! yes, yes, indeed I have kept your face in my mind. Here, here, here!"

And he placed his hand upon his heart.

Suddenly he staggered and turned pale.

"What's the matter?" Arsène inquired in an off-hand way.

"Nothing," replied Hoffmann, "nothing; let us begin."

When he placed his hand on his heart he felt Antonia's locket between his breast and his shirt.

"Let us begin," echoed Arsène. "That's very easy to say. In the first place this isn't the costume that *he* wants me to be painted in."

That word *he*, which she had used twice, pierced Hoffmann's heart like one of the golden pins which secured the modern Aspasia's head-dress.

"How does *he* want you to be painted?" asked Hoffmann with visible bitterness.

"As Erigone."

"Excellent! the head-dress of vine leaves will become you wonderfully."

"Do you think so?" said Arsène, affectedly. "I fancy that the panther's skin won't make me very ugly either."

She struck a bell.

A maid entered.

"Eucharis," said Arsène, "bring the thyrsus, the vine leaves, and the tiger's skin."

She drew out the two or three pins that kept her hair in place, and, with a shake of her head, enveloped herself in billows of black hair which fell in cascades over her shoulders, followed the rounded outline of her hips, and trailed upon the carpet, a dense, wavy mass.

Hoffmann cried out in admiration.

"Well! what is it?" said Arsène.

"Why, I never have seen such hair before!" cried Hoffmann.

"*He* wants me to make the most of it, and that is why *we* chose the costume of Erigone, which allows me to wear my hair loose."

That time the *he* and the *we* dealt Hoffmann's heart two blows instead of one.

Meanwhile Mademoiselle Eucharis had brought the grapes, the thyrsus, and the tiger's skin.

"Is that all we need?" queried Arsène.

"Yes, yes, I think so," stammered Hoffmann.

"Very good; leave us, and don't return until I ring."

Mademoiselle Eucharis went out and closed the door behind her.

"Now, citizen," said Arsène, "just help me to arrange this head-dress; that's your business. I depend a great deal on the painter's taste to make me look well."

"And you are right!" cried Hoffmann. "Mein Gott! mein Gott! how lovely you will be!"

He seized the branch of vine leaves and twined it around Arsène's head with the deft art of the painter, who makes everything contribute to the general effect; and then, shuddering at the first touch, he took the long perfumed hair with the ends of his fingers, intermingled the strands of glossy black with the topaz grapes and the emerald and ruby leaves of the autumn vine; and, as he had promised, under his hand, the hand of a poet, painter, and lover, the dancer's beauty was so enhanced that, upon looking at herself in the mirror, she uttered an exclamation of joy and pride.

"You were right," she said. "Yes, I am beautiful, very beautiful. Now, let us go on."

"What do you say? Let us go on?" queried Hoffmann.

"Why, what about my Bacchante's costume?"

Hoffmann began to understand.

"Mein Gott!" he murmured; "mein Gott!"

Arsène smilingly unfastened her purple cloak, until it was secured only by a single pin, which she tried in vain to reach.

"Why don't you help me?" she said impatiently, "or must I call Eucharis?"

"No, no!" cried Hoffmann. He darted to her side and removed the rebellious pin. The cloak fell at the beautiful Greek's feet.

"There!" said the young man, drawing a long breath.

"Tell me," said Arsène, "do you think the tiger's skin will look well over this long muslin dress? I don't think it will, for my part. Besides, *he* wants a genuine Bacchante, not as you see them on the stage, but as they are in Carrache's and Albano's pictures."

"Why, the Bacchantes are nude in Carrache's and Albano's pictures!" cried Hoffmann.

"Well! that's the way *he* wants me, except for the tiger's skin which you can drape as you choose; that's your business."

As she spoke she loosened the ribbon at her waist and unfastened the clasp at her neck, so that the dress slipped down the full length of her lovely body, leaving it bare, as it dropped from her shoulders to her feet.

"Oh!" said Hoffmann, falling on his knees, "this is no mortal, but a goddess."

Arsène pushed the dress and the cloak away with her foot. Then she took up the tiger's skin.

"Come, what do we do with this?" she said. "Pray help me, citizen painter, I am not accustomed to dressing alone."

The ingenuous danseuse called it dressing.

Hoffmann drew near, walking unsteadily, drunken, dazzled, took the tiger's skin, clasped its golden claws around the Bacchante's shoulders, bade his sit, or rather recline on the couch of red cashmere, where she seemed a statue of Parian marble save for the rise and fall of her bosom and the smile upon her lips.

"Am I in a good position?" she asked, putting her arm under her head, and taking a bunch of grapes which she seemed to press against her lips.

"Oh! yes, lovely, lovely, lovely!" whispered Hoffmann. And the lover carried the day over the painter. He fell on his knees, and with a movement swift as thought seized Arsène's hand and covered it with kisses.

She withdrew her hand, more in surprise than wrath.

"Well! what in heaven's name are you doing?" she asked the young man.

The question was asked in such a calm, cool tone, that Hoffmann staggered back, pressing his hands against his temples.

"Nothing, nothing," he faltered. "Forgive me, I am going mad."

"I should think you were," said she.

"Tell me," cried Hoffmann, "why did you send for me? Tell me, tell me!"

"Why, to have you paint my portrait, and for nothing else."

"Ah! yes," said Hoffmann. "Yes, you are right; to paint your portrait, nothing else."

Making a mighty effort to recover his self-possession, Hoffmann placed his canvas on his easel, took his palette and his brushes, and began to sketch the intoxicating picture that he had before his eyes.

But he had presumed too far upon his strength. When he saw his voluptuous model posing, not simply in her glowing reality, but reflected a thousand times by the innumerable mirrors in the boudoir; when he found himself in the presence of ten Bacchantes instead of one Erigone; when he saw reflected in each mirror that intoxicating smile, the undulations of that breast which the tiger's golden skin only half covered, he felt that he was called upon to exert more than human self-control, and, dashing down his palette and brushes, he rushed at the beautiful Bacchante and imprinted on her shoulder a kiss in which there was as much frenzied passion as love.

But at that very instant the door was thrown open, and the nymph Eucharis rushed into the boudoir, crying, —

"He! he! he!"

Instantly, before he had time to collect his thoughts, Hoffmann was pushed out of the boudoir by the two women, and the door closed behind him; and, veritably mad with love and rage and jealousy, he staggered through the salon, slid down the stair-rail rather than descended the stairs, and found himself, with no idea how he came there, in the street, having left in Arsène's boudoir his brushes, his box of colors, and his palette, which were nothing, and his hat, which might prove to be much.

XIV.

THE TEMPTER.

WHAT rendered Hoffmann's situation even more lamentable was that his grief was coupled with humiliation; that it was perfectly evident that he had not been summoned by Arsène as a man whom she had noticed at the Opéra, but purely and simply as a painter, a portrait-painting machine, a mirror that reflects the bodies placed before it. Hence Arsène's unmoved manner of removing all her garments, one after another, in his presence; hence her amazement when he kissed her hand; hence her wrath when, in the midst of the burning kiss with which he had reddened her shoulder, he told her that he loved her.

Indeed, was it not stark madness for him, a simple German student, who had come to Paris with three or four hundred thalers, a sum hardly sufficient to pay for the carpet in her reception-room, — was it not madness for him to aspire to that fashionable danseuse, the mistress of the extravagant and voluptuous Danton? That woman was not to be moved by ringing words but by the ring of gold. Her favored lover was not the one who loved her best, but the one who paid the highest price. Let Hoffmann have more money than Danton and Danton would be shown the door when Hoffmann arrived.

Meanwhile it was an undeniable fact that the one who had been shown the door was not Danton but Hoffmann.

Hoffmann returned to his little room, humbler and more melancholy than he had ever been.

So long as he had not been face to face with Arsène, he had had some hope; but the things that he had seen, — her utter indifference to him as a man, the luxurious surroundings in which he had found her, and which were not only her physical life but her moral life, — all those things made it impossible for him even to hope for her unless a vast, unimaginable sum of money should fall into his hands, that is to say, unless a miracle should happen.

So he returned to his lodgings, utterly crushed. His strange passion for Arsène, a passion that was entirely physical and magnetic, and into which the heart did not enter, had manifested itself thus far in fierce, feverish excitement.

Now, that excitement was changed to profound prostration.

A single hope remained, — to find the doctor again and ask his opinion as to what he should do, although there was something extraordinary, fantastic, supernatural about the man, which made him feel that, whenever he was with him, he left real life behind and entered into a sort of dream where neither his will power nor his freedom of action accompanied him, and where he became the plaything of a world that existed for him but not for other people.

So he returned to the wine-shop on Rue de la Monnaie at the usual hour on the following day; but to no purpose did he envelop himself in a cloud of smoke. No face resembling the doctor's appeared to him therein. To no purpose did he close his eyes. When he opened them no one was sitting on the stool he had placed on the other side of the table.

A week passed thus.

On the eighth day Hoffmann, having lost patience, left the wine-shop an hour earlier than usual, that is to say, about four in the afternoon, and walked mechanically toward Rue Saint-Honoré by Saint-Germain-l'Auxerrois and the Louvre.

He had hardly reached that thoroughfare when he noticed a great commotion in the direction of the cemetery des Innocents, and that it seemed to be approaching Place du Palais-Royal. He remembered what had happened on the day following his arrival in Paris, and recognized the same sounds, the same uproar that had made a deep impression on him at the time of Madame du Barry's execution. It was, in fact, the tumbrils from the Conciergerie, on their way to Place de la Révolution, laden with the condemned of the day.

We know Hoffmann's horror of the spectacle; and so, as the tumbrils rapidly advanced he darted into a café on the corner of Rue de la Loi, turned his back to the street, closed his eyes, and put his hands over his ears, for Madame du Barry's shrieks were still echoing in the depths of his heart. Then, when he supposed that the tumbrils had passed, he turned, and to his unbounded amazement saw his friend Zacharias Werner stepping down from a chair which he had mounted in order to see better.

"Werner!" cried Hoffmann, rushing up to him, "Werner!"

"Hallo, is it you?" said the poet. "Where were you?"

"I was here, but I had my hands over my ears so as not to hear the shrieks of those poor wretches, and my eyes closed so as not to see them."

"Really, my dear friend, you make a mistake," said

Werner, "for you are a painter! And what you would have seen would have furnished you with a subject for a fine picture. There was a woman in the third tumbril, a wonderful creature, with such a neck and shoulders and hair! cut off behind, to be sure, but falling to the ground on both sides."

"Look you," said Hoffmann. "I saw the finest picture that could be seen of that kind. I saw Madame du Barry, and I do not need to see any others. If I ever want to paint a picture, believe me, that sight will be enough for me; but I don't propose to paint any more pictures."

"Why not?" queried Werner.

"I have conceived a perfect horror of painting."

"Some fresh disappointment?"

"My dear Werner, I shall go mad if I stay in Paris."

"You will go mad wherever you are, my dear Hoffmann. You might as well be in Paris as anywhere else. Meanwhile tell me what it is that is driving you mad."

"Oh! my dear Werner, I am in love."

"With Antonia, I know. So you told me."

"No," said Hoffmann, with a start. "No, that's a different matter. I love Antonia!"

"The devil! it's a subtle distinction. Tell me about it. Citizen official, some beer and glasses!"

The two young men filled their pipes, and seated themselves on opposite sides of a table in the darkest corner of the café.

There Hoffmann told Werner all that had happened to him, from the day that he went to the Opéra and saw Arsène dance, down to the moment when the two women pushed him out of the boudoir.

"Well?" said Werner, when Hoffmann had finished.

"Well!" echoed Hoffmann, amazed that his friend was not as downcast as himself.

"I ask you," continued Werner, "what there is so desperate in all that?"

"Why, my dear fellow, now that I know that the woman can be won only by money, I have lost all hope."

"Why have you lost all hope?"

"Because I shall never have five hundred louis to throw at her feet."

"Why should n't you have them? For my part, I have had five hundred louis, yes, a thousand, two thousand."

"Where do you suppose I am to get them? Great God!" cried Hoffmann.

"Why, at the Eldorado I told you of, at the source of the river Pactolus, my dear fellow, at the gaming-table."

"At the gaming-table!" exclaimed Hoffmann with a shudder. "Why, you know that I swore to Antonia that I would n't gamble."

"Bah!" laughed Werner. "You also swore that you would be true to her!"

Hoffmann heaved a deep sigh, and pressed the locket against his heart.

"At the gaming-table, my friend!" continued Werner. "Ah! that's the bank for you! It is n't like the bank at Mannheim or Homburg, that threatens to break for a few paltry thousands. A million, my boy! a million! stacks of gold! I believe that all the legal tender in France has taken shelter there. None of your wretched paper money, none of your vile, demone-tized assignats, which are worth only a fourth of their face value, but noble louis, noble double louis, noble quadruples! Look, do you want to see some?"

And Werner drew from his pocket a handful of louis and showed them to Hoffmann. Their golden beams flashed through the mirror of his eyes to the inmost recesses of his brain.

"Oh, no! no! never!" he cried, remembering at the same moment the old officer's prediction and Antonia's prayer. "I will never gamble!"

"You are wrong. With such luck as you have you would break the bank."

"And Antonia! Antonia!"

"Bah! my dear friend, who will tell Antonia that you gambled, that you won a million? Who will tell her that, with twenty-five thousand francs you gratified your fancy for the fair ballet-dancer? Believe me, when you return to Mannheim with nine hundred and seventy-five thousand, Antonia will never ask you where you got your forty-eight thousand a year, nor what you did with the other fifteen thousand."

As he spoke, Werner rose.

"Where are you going?" Hoffmann asked him.

"I am going to see a mistress of mine, a lady at the Comédie-Française, who honors me with her favor, and whom I subsidize with half of my winnings. Dame! I am a poet, so I turn my attention to a literary theatre. You are a musician, and you make your choice at a singing and dancing theatre. Good luck at play, my dear friend. My compliments to Mademoiselle Arsène. Don't forget the number of the bank; it is 113. Farewell."

"Ah!" muttered Hoffmann, "you told me that before, and I have n't forgotten it."

He allowed his friend to depart, having neglected again, as at their first meeting, to ask him for his address.

But, although Werner had left him, Hoffmann was not alone. Every word his friend uttered was visible to him and palpable, so to speak. They glistened in his eyes and whispered in his ears.

In very truth, where could Hoffmann go to obtain gold, if not to the golden spring? Had he not found the only possible means of gratifying an impossible longing? Ah! yes, Werner had said truly. Had he not already been false to a part of his oath? What mattered it then if he should be false to the other part?

And again, as Werner had said, he might win not twenty-five thousand, not fifty thousand, not a hundred thousand, but a million francs. The material horizons of fields, woods, and seas have limits. The horizon of the green cloth has none.

The demon of play is like Satan. It has the power of carrying the gambler to the top of the highest mountain on earth, and there pointing out to him all the kingdoms of the world.

And what happiness, what bliss, what pride would be his when he should return to Arsène, to the same boudoir from which he had been thrust out! With what supreme disdain he would crush that woman and her terrible lover, when, for all reply to the words, "Why are you here?" he, another Jupiter, should pour down a shower of gold upon that other Danaë!

And all this was no longer an hallucination of his mind, a dream of his imagination, but it was reality; it was possible. The chances of winning and losing were even. Aye, those of winning were the greater, for, as we know, Hoffmann was lucky at play.

Oh! that number 113, that number 113, with its glowing figures, how it beckoned to Hoffmann, how it showed the way, an infernal beacon-light, to the abyss

in whose depths the demon Vertigo roars, writhing upon
a couch of gold!

Hoffmann struggled for more than an hour against the
fiercest of all passions. Then at the end of that hour,
feeling that it was impossible for him to resist longer,
he tossed a fifteen-sous piece on the table, making the
waiter a gift of the change, and ran without stopping
for breath to Quai aux Fleurs, went up to his room,
took the three hundred thalers he still possessed, and,
without giving himself time for reflection, leaped into
a cab, shouting, —

"To Palais-Égalité!"

XV.

NUMBER 113.

THE Palais-Royal, which was called at that time Palais-Égalité, and which has also been called Palais-National, — for, with us, the first thing that revolutionists do is change the names of streets and squares, so that they can be changed back again when the revolution is at an end, — the Palais-Royal, we say, under which name it is most familiar to us, was not at that time what it is to-day; but in the matter of picturesqueness, and of strangeness too, it was in no wise inferior, especially in the evening, especially at the hour when Hoffmann arrived there.

Its arrangement differed little from what we see to-day, with the exception that what is now called the Galerie d'Orléans was then a double-roofed gallery, which was to give place later to a promenade with six rows of Doric columns; that there were chestnuts instead of lindens in the garden, and that, where the basin now is, there was a circus, a vast structure with walls of trellis-work, bordered with glass, and with shrubs and flowers on the summit.

Do not imagine that that circus was at all the same as the place of amusement to which we in our day have given the name. No, the acrobats and magicians who performed their feats in the Circus at the Palais-Égalité were of a different species from Monsieur Price, who, a few years ago, set France agog and gave birth to the Mazuriers and Auriols.

The Circus was occupied at the time of which we write by the "Friends of Truth," who gave performances there, and whose performances could be witnessed by any one who was a subscriber to the "Bouche de Fer" newspaper. With its number for the morning as a talisman, you were admitted in the evening to that abode of pleasure, and could listen there to the harangues of all the brethren, who were associated together, so they said, with the laudable purpose of protecting governors and governed, of making the laws impartial, and of going to every corner of the world in search of a friend of truth, whatever his nationality, whatever his color, whatever his opinions; and when the truth was discovered, they would reveal it to mankind.

As you see, there have always been men in France who were fully persuaded that it was their mission to enlighten the masses, and that the rest of mankind was a horde of absurd, useless creatures.

What has the passing breeze done with the names and ideas and vain pretensions of those people?

However the Circus made a noise of its own in the Palais-Égalité amid the general uproar there, and mingled its shrill notes in the grand concert that was performed every evening in that garden.

For it should be said that, in those days of privation, exile, terror, and proscription, the Palais-Royal had become the great centre to which the life that was repressed all day by political passions and struggles, resorted at night, in search of distraction and to do its utmost to forget the truth which the members of the Cercle Social and the stockholders of the Circus had set out to find. While all the quarters of Paris were dark and deserted; while the ominous patrols, composed of the jailers of to-day and the executioners of to-morrow, prowled about like wild beasts in quest of any sort of prey; while, around the fireside of a dead or outlawed friend or parent, those who were left sadly exchanged in whispers their fears or their sorrows, the Palais-Royal shone like the god of evil. Its hundred and eighty arcades were brilliantly-lighted, it displayed its trinkets in the jewellers' windows, it scattered amid the popular *carmagnoles* and the universal misery its abandoned women, gleaming with diamonds, covered with white and red paint, dressed just as much as they were compelled to be, in silk or velvet, and exhibiting their marvellous shamelessness under the trees and in the galleries. This magnificent prostitution was a last withering satire upon the past, a last insult to the monarchy.

To display those creatures in their royal costumes was to throw mud after blood in the faces of that court of lovely, luxury-loving women, of whom Marie-Antoinette was the queen, and whom the revolutionary whirlwind had swept from the Trianon to Place de la Révolution, — as if a drunken man should drag his fiancée's white dress in the mire.

Luxury was abandoned to the vilest prostitutes; virtue was fated to go clad in rags.

That was one of the truths discovered by the Cercle Social.

But the people that had given the world such a violent forward impulse, the Parisian people, in whom, unluckily, reasoning always comes after enthusiasm, — the result being that they are never cool-blooded enough to remember the foolish things they have done, — the people, we say, being poor and in rags, did not altogether understand the philosophy of that antithesis, and it was with envy, not with contempt, that they rubbed elbows with those brothel-queens, those ghastly sovereigns of vice. And when, their passions excited by what they saw, when, with their eyes on fire, they sought to lay their hands upon those bodies that belonged to the whole world, they were called upon for money, and, having none, were ignominiously repulsed. Thus was the great principle of equality mocked at everywhere, — the great principle, which was proclaimed by the axe, written in blood, and which the prostitutes of the Palais-Royal were entitled to spit upon.

In days like those, mental invigoration reached such a point that such extraordinary contrasts were necessary to the reality of things. People were dancing not on the volcano, but in the crater itself, and their lungs, being accustomed to an atmosphere of sulphur and lava, were no longer content with the mild perfumes of other days.

Thus the Palais-Royal reared its head every evening, illuminating everything with its crown of flame. A procurer in stone, it shouted over the great, sorrowing city : —

"It is night, come! I have everything within my walls, fortune and love, gaming and women! I sell everything, even suicide and murder. Ye who have eaten nothing since yesterday, ye who suffer, ye who weep, come to me. Ye shall see how rich we are; ye shall see how we laugh! Have ye a conscience or a daughter to sell? Come! your eyes shall be filled with gold, your ears with obscenity. Ye shall wade to your knees in vice, in corruption, and in oblivion. Come here to-night, perhaps ye will be dead men to-morrow."

That last was the great argument. One must live as one was likely to die, rapidly.

And they came.

The most frequented spot of all was naturally that

where there was gambling. That was the place to obtain the means of enjoying the rest.

And so, of all those brilliant dens, number 113 was the one that cast the most brilliant light, with its red lantern, the huge eye of the Cyclops called Palais-Égalité.

If hell has a number, that number should be 113.

Ah! all one's wants were anticipated there.

On the ground-floor there was a restaurant. On the first floor there were the gambling-rooms. The breast of the building contained the heart, as was quite natural. And that was the house to which Hoffmann, Antonia's poetic lover, was hurrying with all speed.

Number 113 was where it is to-day, a few doors from the Maison Corcelet.

Hoffmann had no sooner alighted from his carriage and set his foot inside the gallery of the palace, than he was accosted by the divinities of the place, thanks to his foreign costume, which, in those days as in our own, inspired more confidence than the national costume.

A country is never so much despised as by itself.

"Where is number 113?" Hoffmann inquired of the damsel who had taken his arm.

"Oh! that's where you're going," said Aspasia, disdainfully. "Well, my lad, it's where you see that red lantern. But try to keep two louis and remember number 115."

Hoffmann plunged into the passage-way pointed out to him as Curtius plunged into the gulf, and a moment later he was in the card-room.

There was the same noise as in a public auction-room.

To be sure many things were sold there.

The rooms were resplendent with gilding, chandeliers,

flowers, and women more beautiful, more richly dressed, and more décolletées than those below.

The noise that dominated all the other noises was the chink of gold. It was the heart-beat of that degraded multitude.

Hoffmann left at his right the room where *trente et quarante* was in progress, and passed on to the *salon de roulette*.

Around a large green table sat the players, all of whom were assembled for the same purpose, and no two of whom wore the same expression.

There were young and old; there were some whose elbows were worn through by leaning on that table. Among the men there were those who had lost their fathers the day before or that morning or that very evening, and whose thoughts were all absorbed by the revolving ball. In the true gambler a single sentiment continues to live, — desire; and that sentiment is nourished and increases in force at the expense of all others. Monsieur de Bassompierre, who was told that his mother was dead as he was about to dance with Marie de Médici, and who replied, " My mother will not die until I have danced," — Monsieur de Bassompierre was a devoted son compared to a gambler. A gambler actually at play, to whom such a remark should be made, would not even answer as Monsieur de Bassompierre did: in the first place, because it would be a waste of time, and in the second place, a gambler, if he never has a heart, ceases to have a mind when he is gambling. And when he is not gambling it is the same thing, he is thinking about it.

The gambler has all the virtues of his vice. He is sober, he is patient, he is indefatigable. A gambler who could abruptly turn aside to the profit of an hon

orable passion or a noble sentiment, the incredible energy
that he places at the disposal of his passion for play,
would instantly become one of the greatest men in the
world. Never did Cæsar, Hannibal, or Napoleon, even
when earnestly engaged in performing their greatest
manœuvres, display a force of will equal to that of the
obscurest gambler. Ambition, love, passion, the heart,
the mind, the sense of hearing, the sense of smell, the
sense of touch, all the mainsprings of man's life, in fact,
are united upon a single word, a single purpose, — gambling. And do not imagine that the gambler plays to
win. He begins that way, but he ends by gambling for
gambling's sake, in order to see the cards, to handle
gold, to feel the strange emotions that have not their
like in any of the other passions of life, emotions which,
in the face of gain or loss, — those two poles from one
to the other of which the gambler flies with the speed
of the wind, one of which burns like fire and the other
freezes like ice, — cause his heart to leap within his
breast under the stimulus of desire or reality, as a horse
leaps under the spur; in order to absorb like a sponge
all the faculties of the mind, to confine them and hold
them in check, and, when the hand is played, to release
them abruptly only to seize them again with more force
than before.

The one circumstance that makes the passion for
gambling stronger than all other passions is that, as it
is never satisfied, it can never grow weary. It is like
a mistress who always promises and never gives. It
kills, but it does not fatigue.

The passion for gambling is the hysteria of mankind.

To the gambler everything is dead, family, friends,
country. His horizon is limited by the card and ball.
His country is the chair he sits in, the green cloth on

which he leans. If he were condemned to the gridiron
like St. Lawrence, and were allowed to gamble there, I
am prepared to wager that he would not feel the fire,
that he would not even turn his head.

The gambler is a silent creature. Words can be of no
service to him. He plays, he wins, he loses. He is no
longer a man; he is a machine. Why should he speak?

The uproar in the card-rooms did not come from the
players, therefore, but from the croupiers, who raked in
the gold and cried in nasal tones, —

" Make your bets ! "

At that moment Hoffmann was no longer an observer.
His passion had taken too full possession of him.
Otherwise he could have made a whole series of interest-
ing studies.

He glided rapidly through the spectators and reached
the edge of the green cloth. He found himself between
a man in a *carmagnole* who was standing, and an old
man who was sitting down and making calculations on a
piece of paper.

The old man, who had spent his life seeking a successful combination, was spending his last days in
playing it, and his last louis in seeing it fail. The
successful combination is as impossible to find as the
soul.

Among the heads of the men, sitting and standing,
appeared the heads of women who were leaning on their
shoulders, dabbling their hands in their gold, and who,
with unequalled dexterity, found a way to profit by the
winnings of some and the losses of others.

Seeing the cups filled with gold and the pyramids of
silver, one would have found it hard to believe that the
public destitution was so great and that gold was so
dear.

The man in the *carmagnole* tossed a bundle of papers on a number.

"Fifty francs," he said.

"What's that?" asked the croupier, pulling in the papers with his rake, and taking them up with the ends of his fingers.

"*Assignats*," the man replied.

"Haven't you any other money than that?" said the croupier.

"No, citizen."

"Then you can give somebody else your place."

"Why so?"

"Because we don't take that stuff."

"It's government money."

"So much the better for the government if it can use it! We don't want it."

"Upon my word!" rejoined the man, taking up his *assignats*, "this is a wretched kind of money; you can't even lose it."

He walked away, crumpling the *assignats* in his hands.

"Make your bets!" cried the croupier.

Hoffmann was a gambler, as we know; but this time he played, not for the sake of playing, but for the money.

The fever that consumed him kept his thoughts boiling in his mind like water in a kettle.

"A hundred thalers on 26!" he cried.

The croupier scrutinized the German money as he had scrutinized the *assignats*. "Go and change it," he said to Hoffmann. "We take only French money."

Hoffmann ran downstairs like a madman, entered the shop of a money-changer who happened to be a German himself, and exchanged his three hundred thalers for French gold, that is to say, for about forty louis.

The wheel had turned three times meanwhile.

"Fifteen louis on 26!" he cried, rushing to the table, and clinging, with the gambler's extraordinary superstition, to the number he had chosen at first by chance, simply because the man with the *assignats* had tried to bet upon it.

"No more bets!" cried the croupier.

The ball went on its way.

Hoffmann's neighbor picked up two handfuls of gold and tossed them into his hat, which he held between his legs, but the croupier raked in Hoffmann's fifteen louis and many others.

Number 16 had won.

Hoffmann felt the cold perspiration overspread his brow like a net with steel meshes.

"Fifteen louis on 26!" he repeated.

Other voices called out other numbers, and the wheel turned once more.

On that turn the bank won everything. The ball rolled into the zero.

"Ten louis on 26!" muttered Hoffmann in a choking voice; but, thinking better of it, he said, "no, only nine," and took back one gold piece in order to have one more chance to play, one last hope.

Number 30 won.

The gold was swept from the cloth like the waves that beat high upon the shore, and are swept back into the sea.

Hoffmann, whose heart was beating fiercely, and who saw through the mists in his brain Arsène's mocking smile and Antonia's sad features, — Hoffmann, we say, with trembling hand, placed his last louis upon 26.

The bets were made in a moment.

"No more bets!" cried the croupier.

Hoffmann followed with a gleaming eye the rolling ball, as if it were his own life that was rolling over and over before his eyes.

Suddenly he threw himself back, hiding his face in his hands.

Not only had he lost, but he had not a single sou about his person or at his lodgings.

A woman who sat near by, and who would have sold herself for twenty francs a moment before, uttered a fierce cry of joy and picked up a handful of gold she had won.

Hoffmann would have given ten years of his life for one of that woman's louis.

With a movement swifter than thought he felt and searched his pockets, as if to banish all doubt as to the truth.

His pockets were empty, but he felt something round, like a piece of money against his breast, and eagerly seized it.

It was Antonia's locket, which he had forgotten.

" I am saved ! " he cried; and he threw the locket as a stake upon number 26.

XVI.

THE LOCKET.

THE croupier took the locket and examined it.

"Monsieur," he said to Hoffmann, for they still said monsieur at 113, "monsieur, go and sell this if you choose, and make your bet in money; but, I tell you once more, we take nothing but gold or silver coin."

Hoffmann took his locket and left the room without uttering a syllable.

During the time that it took him to go down the stairs many thoughts, many plans, many presentiments buzzed around him; but he turned a deaf ear to all those vague sounds, and went directly to the same money-changer who had just given him louis for his thalers.

The good man was reading, lying back comfortably in his leather-covered arm-chair, with his spectacles perched on the end of his nose. He was reading by the uncertain light of a low lamp, reenforced by the yellow glitter of the gold pieces in their copper receptacles, and he was protected by a lattice of fine iron wire, with little green silk curtains, and a little wicket, only large enough for the hand to pass through, on a level with the table.

Hoffmann had never felt such an overpowering admiration for gold.

He opened his eyes, marvelling greatly, as if he had stepped into a sunbeam, and yet he had just seen more gold on the roulette table than he saw there; but it was not the same kind of gold, philosophically speaking.

Between the noisy, swift-moving, excited gold at number 113, and the tranquil, silent, serious gold at the money-changer's, there was the same difference that there is between vapid, empty-headed chatterers and men of thought and meditation. A man can do no good with the gold won at roulette or cards. It does not belong to him in whose possession it is, but he belongs to it. Coming from a corrupt source, it must serve an impure end. It has life in it, but it is a vicious life, and it is in haste to be gone as it came. It counsels naught but vice, and, when it does do good, does it against its will. It arouses longings ten times, twenty times greater than it can satisfy, and, when you once possess it, it seems to diminish in value. In a word, the money of the gaming-table always has a fictitious value, depending upon whether one wins or longs to win or loses. Sometimes a handful of gold represents nothing; sometimes a single coin contains a man's life; whereas the gold of commerce, the gold of the money-changer, gold like that which Hoffmann went to his compatriot to obtain, is always worth its face value. It leaves its copper nest only in exchange for something of equal or superior value to itself. It does not prostitute itself by passing from hand to hand like a courtesan without shame, without preference, without love. It has respect for itself. When it has once left the money-changer's hands it may become corrupted; it may keep bad company, as it may have done before going there, but while it is there it is respectable and deserving of consideration. It is the image of need and not of caprice. You earn it; you do not win it. It is not tossed about like mere counters by the croupiers, but is slowly and carefully counted, piece by piece, by the broker, with all the respect that is its due. It is silent and in that its great eloquence consists; and so Hoffmann, through whose imagination a comparison of this sort flashed in a moment's time, began to tremble lest the broker should refuse to give him such genuine gold for his locket. He deemed himself obliged, therefore, although it involved a loss of valuable time, to resort to periphrases and circumlocution to arrive at his goal, especially as he had not come to propose a business transaction to the money-changer, but to ask a favor at his hands.

"Monsieur," he said, "I came here a short time ago to exchange thalers for louis."

"Yes, monsieur, I recognize you," said the money-changer.

"You are a German?"

"I am from Heidelberg."

"That is where I studied."

"What a beautiful town!"

"It is, indeed."

Meanwhile Hoffmann's blood was boiling. It seemed to him that every moment he gave to that commonplace conversation was a year of his life thrown away.

He continued, therefore, with a smile, —

"I thought that perhaps you would be willing, being a fellow-countryman, to do me a favor."

"What is it?" asked the money-changer, his face clouding at the word. The money-changer is no more of a lender than the ant.

"To loan me three louis on this gold locket."

As he spoke, Hoffmann handed the locket to the broker, who put it in his scales and weighed it.

"Wouldn't you prefer to sell it?" he asked.

"Oh! no," cried Hoffmann; "it is bad enough to pawn it. I will even venture to ask you, if you do me this favor, to keep the locket with the greatest care, for I care more for it than for my life, and I shall come and redeem it to-morrow. Nothing less serious than my present circumstances would induce me to pawn it."

"Then I will loan you three louis."

And the money-changer, with all the gravity that such an act seemed to him to require, took three louis and placed them in front of Hoffmann.

"Oh! thanks, thanks a thousand times!" cried Hoffmann, as he pounced upon the three gold pieces and disappeared.

The money-changer silently resumed his reading, after placing the locket in a corner of his drawer. It had never occurred to him to go and venture his gold against other gold at 113.

The gambler is so near being a sacrilegist that Hoffmann, as he tossed his first piece of gold upon number 26, — for he proposed to risk only one at a time, — pronounced the name of Antonia.

While the ball was rolling Hoffmann was not excited. Something told him that he should win.

Number 26 came up.

Hoffmann, beaming with joy, gathered up thirty-six louis.

The first thing that he did was to put three of them aside in his watch-pocket, in order to be sure that he could redeem his fiancée's locket, for he evidently owed his first gains to her. He left thirty-three louis on the same number, and the same number came up. Therefore he won thirty-three times thirty-six, or eleven hundred and eighty-eight louis, that is to say, nearly twenty-five thousand francs.

Thereupon Hoffmann plunged his hands into that solid Pactolus, and, taking it up by handfuls, played at random, blinded as if by a dazzling light. At every play that he made, his heap of winnings increased, like a mountain suddenly rising from the water.

He had gold in his pockets, in his coat, in his waistcoat, in his hat, in his hands, on the table, everywhere. Gold rolled to him from the croupier's hands like blood from a gaping wound. He had become the Jupiter of all the Danaës in the room, and the treasurer of all the unlucky players.

At last, when he thought that he had enough, he picked up all the gold in front of him and fled in the direction of Arsène's house, leaving all his fellow-gamblers full of admiration and envy.

It was one o'clock in the morning; but it mattered little to him.

It seemed to him that with such wealth he might come at any hour of the night and always be sure of a welcome.

He gloated over the thought of covering with all that gold the beautiful body which had unveiled itself before him, and which, although it had remained as cold as marble to his love, would awake to life before his wealth, like the statue modelled by Prometheus when he had found its animating principle.

He proposed to go to Arsène, to empty his pockets to the last piece, and say to her, "Now, love me." Then, the next day, he would leave Paris, in order to escape, if possible, the memory of that intense, feverish dream.

He knocked at Arsène's door like a master returning to his own house.

The door opened.

Hoffmann ran to the stairs.

"Who is that?" cried the concierge's voice.

Hoffmann did not reply.

"Where are you going, citizen?" said the same voice; and a ghost, dressed as ghosts are at night, came out of the lodge and ran after Hoffmann.

In those days people were very fond of knowing who went out and especially who came in.

"I am going to Mademoiselle Arsène's," replied Hoffmann, tossing the concierge three or four louis, for which an hour earlier he would have sold his soul.

That method of expression was very satisfactory to the official.

"Mademoiselle Arsène is no longer here, monsieur," he replied, deeming it advisable to use some other word than "citizen" when he had to do with so open-handed a man. A man who asks may say, "citizen;" but a man who receives can say only "monsieur."

"What!" cried Hoffmann, "Arsène not here?"

"No, monsieur."

"You mean that she hasn't come home this evening?"

"I mean that she won't come any more."

"Where is she, then?"

"I have no idea."

"*Mein Gott! mein Gott!*" exclaimed Hoffmann; and he took his head in his hands as if to hold back his reason, which was on the point of escaping him. Everything that had happened to him of late was so extraordinary that he kept saying to himself, "There, now I am going mad!"

"Haven't you heard the news?" said the concierge.

"What news?"

"Monsieur Danton has been arrested."

"When?"

"Yesterday. It was Monsieur Robespierre who did it. A great man, Citizen Robespierre!"

"Well?"

"Well, Mademoiselle Arsène was obliged to fly; for, as Danton's mistress, she was likely to be compromised in the affair."

"True. But how did she fly?"

"As one flies when one is afraid of having his head cut off, — straight before her."

"Thanks, my friend, thanks," said Hoffmann; and he disappeared, leaving a few more gold pieces in the concierge's hand.

When he was in the street, Hoffmann asked himself the question, what was going to become of him, and of what use all his gold was to him now; for, as may be imagined, the idea that he could find Arsène never occurred to him, any more than the idea of going home and taking some rest.

So he too began to walk straight before him, making the pavements of the deserted streets ring beneath his heels, wide awake, and yet dreaming a painful dream.

It was a cold night. The trees were bare and shivered in the night wind, like sick men in delirium who have left their beds, and whose wasted limbs are shaken by fever.

The frost stung the faces of the few nocturnal passers-by, and only at long intervals was the darkness pierced by a light in a window of one of the houses whose black masses could hardly be distinguished from the sky.

But the cold air had a salutary effect upon him. His heart expanded gradually in that rapid walk, and, if we may so express ourselves, his mental effervescence was volatilized. In a room he would have stifled. And then, perhaps, if he went on and on, he might fall in with Arsène. Who could say? Perhaps when she fled from her house she had gone in the same direction as he.

22

He walked the whole length of the deserted boulevard and through Rue Royale, as if, knowing that his eyes did not see, his feet had recognized the place where he was. He raised his head, and stopped when he saw that he was going straight toward Place de la Révolution, toward the square to which he had taken an oath never to return.

Dark as was the sky, a silhouette that was even darker stood out against the inky horizon. It was the silhouette of the ghastly machine, whose mouth, wet with blood, was dried by the night wind as it slept, awaiting the coming of its daily quota of victims.

It was by daylight that Hoffmann did not want to see the square. It was because of the blood that flowed there that he desired to avoid it; but at night it was a different matter. To the poet, in whom, despite all that had passed, the poetic instinct was still awake, it was intensely interesting to see and to touch with his hands, in the silence and darkness, the sinister scaffolding whose blood-stained image must have haunted many minds at that period.

What more striking contrast to the tumultuous gambling hell he had just left, than that deserted square whose perpetual guest was the grim scaffold! by day, the spectacle of death; at night, solitude, insensibility!

So Hoffmann walked toward the guillotine as if drawn thither by a magnetic force.

Suddenly, and almost without knowing how it had come about, he found himself face to face with it.

The wind was whistling through the boards.

Hoffmann folded his arms across his breast and looked.

How many thoughts must have been born in the mind of that young man, who, with his pockets filled with gold, after reckoning upon a night of debauchery, was passing the night alone beside a scaffold!

It seemed to him, in the midst of his reverie, as if a human groan were mingled with the sighing of the wind.

He leaned his head forward and listened.

The groan was repeated, not at a distance, but near the ground.

He looked about and saw no one.

Meanwhile a third groan reached his ears.

"One would say it was a woman's voice," he muttered, "and it seems to come from beneath the scaffold."

Stooping down, in order to see better, he began to make the circuit of the guillotine. As he passed the terrible ladder, his foot stumbled against something. He put out his hands and touched a human body, dressed entirely in black, crouching on the lower step.

"Who are you, who sleep beside a scaffold at night?" asked Hoffmann.

And as he spoke he knelt in order to see the face of the person to whom he was speaking.

But she did not stir. Her elbows were resting on her knees, and her head upon her hands.

Despite the bitter cold her shoulders were almost entirely bare, and Hoffmann could see a black line around her white neck.

That line was a velvet necklace.

"Arsène!" he cried.

"Ah! yes, I am Arsène!" muttered the crouching woman in a strange voice, as she raised her head and looked at Hoffmann.

XVII.

A HOTEL ON RUE SAINT-HONORÉ.

HOFFMANN recoiled in terror. Despite the voice, despite the face, he still doubted. But Arsène raised her head and let her hands fall upon her knees, thus uncovering her neck and disclosing the curious diamond clasp that secured the ends of the velvet necklace; and it sparkled in the darkness.

"Arsène! Arsène!" Hoffmann repeated.

Arsène rose.

"What are you doing here at this hour," the young man asked, "clad in this black dress, with your shoulders bare."

"He was taken away yesterday," Arsène replied. "They came to arrest me too. I fled just as I was, and to-night, as my room seemed too small and my bed too cold, I came out at eleven o'clock and found my way here."

The words were uttered in a strange voice, without inflection, without gestures. They issued from pallid lips which opened and closed as if by a spring. One would have said that an automaton was speaking.

"But you cannot remain here!" cried Hoffmann.

"Where should I go? I cannot return to the place I came from, until the last moment. It was too cold."

"Then come with me," cried Hoffmann.

"With you!" exclaimed Arsène.

And it seemed to the young man that a disdainful glance fell upon him in the starlight from that dull eye,

like the glance that had crushed him in the lovely
boudoir on Rue de Hanovre.

"I am rich; I have gold," cried Hoffmann.

The dancer's eye flashed.

"Come," she said, "but where?"

"*Where?*"

Indeed, *where* was he to take that woman of luxurious, voluptuous tastes, who, when she had left the
magnificent palaces and enchanted gardens of the Opéra,
was accustomed to walk upon Persian carpets and to
recline upon Indian cashmeres?

Certainly he could not take her to his little student's
chamber. She would be as stifled and as cold there as
in the unknown abode of which she just spoke, and to
which she seemed to dread to return.

"Where, indeed?" said Hoffmann. "I am a
stranger in Paris."

"I will show you where to go," said Arsène.

"Oh! yes, yes," cried Hoffmann.

"Follow me."

She started off in front of him at a swift, automatic
gait which had nothing in common with the charming
suppleness he had admired in the dancer.

It did not occur to the young man to offer her his
arm. He followed her.

Arsène turned into Rue Royale, which was called at
that time Rue de la Révolution, turned to the right
into Rue Saint-Honoré, which was called Rue Honoré
without the prefix, stopped in front of a magnificent
hotel and rang.

The door was opened at once.

The concierge gazed at Arsène in open-mouthed
amazement.

"Speak to him," she said to the young man, "or they

won't let me go in, and I shall be obliged to return to my seat at the foot of the guillotine."

"My friend," said Hoffmann, hastily, passing between the concierge and the young woman, "as I was passing along Champs-Élysées, I heard some one calling for help. I ran up in time to prevent madame from being murdered, but too late to prevent her being robbed. Give me your best room at once. Have a great fire lighted in it, and serve a good supper. Here's a louis for you."

He cast a louis d'or on the table on which the lamp stood, and all the rays of light seemed to concentrate on the gleaming features of Louis XV.

A louis was a large sum at that time. It represented nine hundred and twenty-five francs in *assignats*.

The concierge removed his dirty cap and rang. A waiter answered the bell.

"Quick! quick! a room, the best in the house, for monsieur and madame!"

"For monsieur and madame," repeated the waiter, staring in open-mouthed wonder at Hoffmann's more than simple dress and Arsène's more than airy costume, one after the other.

"Yes," said Hoffmann, "the best, the finest; and above all things let it be well warmed and well lighted. Here's a louis for you."

The waiter seemed to undergo the same influence as the concierge, bowed before the louis, and pointed to a grand staircase, which was but half-lighted because of the advanced hour of the night, but which was carpeted from top to bottom, — a most unusual extravagance at that period.

"Go up," he said, "and wait at the door of number three."

With that he disappeared.

On the first stair Arsène stopped.

Light-footed sylph though she was, she seemed to find an insuperable difficulty in lifting her foot. You would have said that her thin satin shoes were soled with lead.

Hoffmann offered her his arm. Arsène rested her hand upon it, and although he did not feel the weight of her hand, he was conscious of a sensation of cold from the contact.

With a violent effort Arsène mounted the first stair and the others in succession; but every stair extorted a sigh from her.

" O poor girl! " murmured Hoffmann. " How you must have suffered! "

" Yes, yes," replied Arsène, " I have suffered much."

They reached the door of number three. But the waiter arrived almost as soon as they, bringing a veritable brazier. He opened the door and in an instant a fire was blazing on the hearth, and the candles were lighted.

" You must be hungry, are you not? " Hoffmann asked.

" I don't know," was the reply.

" The best supper you can give us, boy," said Hoffmann.

" Monsieur," said the waiter, " people don't say *boy* nowadays, but *official*. However, monsieur pays so handsomely, that he can say what he chooses."

Delighted with his own wit, he went out, saying, —

" Supper will be ready in five minutes."

When the door had closed behind him, Hoffmann turned and looked at Arsène.

She was in such haste to be near the fire that she had not time to draw an easy-chair to the hearth. She simply crouched in front of it, in the same position in which Hoffmann had found her in front of the guillotine; and there, her elbows resting on her knees, she seemed intent upon holding her head straight upon her shoulders with both hands.

"Arsène, Arsène!" said the young man. "I told you that I was rich, did I not? Look, and you will see that I did not lie."

He began by emptying his hat upon the table. It was filled with louis and double louis, and they poured from it on the marble with the peculiar ringing sound that is so easily distinguished from all other sounds.

Then he emptied his pockets, which, one after another, disgorged the enormous plunder he had bagged at the gaming-table.

A heap of restless, resplendent gold pieces covered the table.

Arsène seemed to come to life at the sound. She turned her head, and what she saw seemed to complete the resurrection begun by what she had heard.

She rose, still stiff and rigid; but her pale lips smiled, her glassy eyes lighted up and shot forth rays that blended with the rays of the gold.

"Oh!" said she. "Is all that yours?"

"No, not mine, but yours, Arsène."

"Mine!" exclaimed the dancer.

She plunged her bloodless hands into the heap of metal. Her arms disappeared to the elbow, and she, whose very life gold had been, seemed to live again at the touch of gold.

"Mine," she said, "mine!" and she uttered the words in a quivering, metallic tone that blended in a most extraordinary way with the chink of the louis.

Two waiters entered, bringing a table all set, which

they were near dropping when they espied the mass of riches the young woman was kneading in her clinched hands.

"Very good," said Hoffmann. "Bring some champagne and leave us."

The waiters brought several bottles of champagne and withdrew.

Hoffmann closed the door behind them and locked it.

Then, his eyes glowing with desire, he returned to Arsène, whom he found standing at the table, renewing her life, not in the fountain of Youth, but in that yellow Pactolus.

"Well!" he said inquiringly.

"Gold is beautiful!" she said. "It is long since I touched any."

"Come and sup," said Hoffmann, "and after supper, if you choose, O Danaë, you shall bathe in gold at your ease."

He led her to the table.

"I am cold!" she said.

Hoffmann looked about the room. There were red damask curtains to the bed and at the windows. He tore a curtain from the window and gave it to Arsène.

She wrapped herself in the curtain, which seemed to drape itself about her in graceful folds like the cloaks worn by the ancient Greeks, and her pale face, surrounded by that red drapery, seemed doubly pale.

Hoffmann was almost afraid.

He took his place at the table, poured and drank two or three glasses of champagne in rapid succession. Thereupon it seemed to him that a slight flush overspread Arsène's cheeks.

He poured wine for her, and she too drank. Then he tried to make her eat. but she refused.

"I could not swallow," she said, when Hoffmann insisted.

"Let us drink then."

"Yes, let us drink," she said, holding out her glass.

Hoffmann was hungry as well as thirsty. He ate and drank.

He drank especially hard. He felt that he needed courage, not that Arsène, as in her own home, seemed disposed to resist him either by force or by contempt, but because there seemed to be an ice-cold emanation from his lovely companion's body.

As he drank, Arsène, in his eyes at least, became more animated; but when she emptied her glass, several red drops rolled from beneath the velvet necklace and trickled down upon the dancer's breast. Hoffmann watched them without understanding; but, feeling that there was some terrible mystery beneath it all, he combated his internal tremors by multiplying toasts to her lovely eyes, her lovely mouth, her lovely hands.

She honored his toasts, drinking as much as he, and seeming to derive animation, not from the wine she drank herself, but from the wine that Hoffmann drank.

Suddenly a stick fell from the fire.

Hoffmann followed with his eyes the blazing brand, which did not stop until it touched Arsène's bare foot. She had removed her shoes and stockings, the better to warm herself, and her little foot, white as marble, rested on the marble hearth, which too was as white as the foot, and seemed to be cut from the same block.

Hoffmann cried out.

"Arsène! Arsène! take care!" he said.

"Of what?" she asked.

"That piece of wood — that wood against your foot."

The brand did, in fact, half cover Arsène's foot.

"Take it away," she said calmly.

Hoffmann stooped, picked up the brand, and discovered, to his intense surprise, that it had not burned the girl's foot, but that the foot had extinguished the flame.

"Let us drink!" said he.

"Let us drink!" said Arsène.

She held out her glass.

The second bottle was empty.

But Hoffmann began to feel that the intoxication of wine was not enough.

His eye fell upon a piano.

"Good!" he exclaimed.

He realized the resource opened to him by the intoxication of music.

He darted to the piano.

Beneath his fingers came forth as naturally as possible the air to which Arsène had danced the *pas de trois* in the opera of the "Judgment of Paris," when he first saw her.

But it seemed to Hoffmann as if the chords of the piano were of steel. The single instrument produced a volume of sound equal to a whole orchestra.

"Ah!" said Hoffmann, "this is glorious!"

He had found in that sound the intoxication he sought.

Arsène rose as he struck the first chords. They seemed to envelop her whole person like a network of flame.

She threw aside the red damask curtain, and, strange to say, just as a magic transformation scene is carried out on the stage, no one knows how, so a transformation took place in her costume, and instead of her black dress and bare shoulders, she appeared in the costume of Flore, bedecked with flowers, enveloped in clouds of gauze, and trembling with excitement.

Hoffmann uttered a sharp exclamation, then played

on with redoubled energy, until the resonant steel muscles in the breast of the instrument seemed instinct with supernatural force.

Thereupon the same hallucination spread confusion in Hoffmann's mind. That pirouetting creature, who had become animated by slow degrees, exerted an irresistible power of attraction over him. She had taken for her stage all the space between the piano and the alcove, and her figure stood out like an apparition from hell against the red background of the bed-curtains. Whenever she returned from the end of the room toward Hoffmann, he rose from his chair. Whenever she moved away from him again, he felt something drawing him after her. At last, — and Hoffmann had no idea how it came about, — the movement changed under his fingers. He no longer played the air he had heard at the Opéra, but a waltz; that waltz was Beethoven's "Desire." It had come naturally to his fingers as an expression of his thought. Arsène too had changed the time of her dance. At first she turned round and round in the same spot, then gradually enlarged the circle she described, and drew nearer and nearer to Hoffmann. Hoffmann, breathing hard, felt her coming, felt her drawing near. He realized that at last she would touch him, and that then he could not resist rising in his turn and taking part in that wild waltz.

He was conscious of a sensation of terror mingled with his passion. At last Arsène, as she passed, put out her hand, and touched him with the ends of her fingers. Hoffmann uttered a cry, jumped as if touched by an electric spark, darted after the dancer, overtook her, threw his arms around her waist, continuing in his thought the air he had ceased to play, clasping to his heart that body which had regained its elasticity, seeking a glance from her eyes, the breath from her mouth, devouring her with kisses; whirling about, no longer in respirable air, but in an atmosphere of flame which penetrated to the deepest recesses of their being, until at last they fell exhausted.

When Hoffmann awoke the next morning, one of the dull days peculiar to a Parisian winter had begun its course, and the light entered the room through the window from which the curtain had been removed. He looked about him, not knowing where he was, and felt a lifeless mass pressing against his left arm. He leaned in the direction from which the numbness that assailed his heart seemed to come, and recognized, lying across the bed, not the lovely danseuse of the Porte Saint-Martin Theatre, but the pallid-faced girl of Place de la Révolution.

Thereupon he remembered everything, and, seeing that the body lay perfectly still, he seized a candlestick in which five candles were still burning, and by their light and the light of day combined, discovered that her face was white and her eyes closed.

His first idea was that fatigue had been too much for her, and that she had fainted. He took her hand; it was as cold as ice. He put his hand over her heart; her heart had ceased to beat.

Thereupon a ghastly thought passed through his mind. He pulled violently at the bell-cord, which broke in his hands. He rushed to the door, opened it, and darted down the stairs, crying, —

"Help! help!"

A little man dressed in black was ascending the stairs at the same moment. He raised his head. Hoffmann looked at him and uttered a cry. He had recognized the physician of the Opéra.

"Ah! is it you, my dear monsieur?" said the doctor as he recognized Hoffmann. "What is the matter, why all this outcry?"

"Oh! come, come," said Hoffmann, not taking the time to explain to his friend what he expected of him, but hoping that the sight of Arsène's inanimate form would have more effect on him than anything he could say. "Come!"

He led him into the room, dragged him to the bed with one hand, and with the other seized the candlestick and held it to Arsène's face.

"Look," he said.

But the doctor, far from manifesting any excitement or dismay, said calmly, —

"Ah! it was well done of you, young man; it was well done of you to redeem the body so that it might not rot in the common trench. Very well done, young man! very well done!"

"The body," muttered Hoffmann, "redeemed, — the common trench! In God's name, what are you talking about?"

"I say that our poor Arsène was arrested yesterday at eight o'clock in the morning, was tried yesterday at two o'clock in the afternoon, and was executed yesterday at four o'clock in the afternoon."

Hoffmann thought that he was going mad. He seized the doctor by the throat.

"Executed yesterday at four o'clock!" he cried, as if he himself were being strangled, "Arsène executed!"

He laughed aloud, but his laugh was so strange, so strident, so utterly distinct from all the ordinary modulations of the human voice, that the doctor glanced at him with something like terror in his eyes.

"Do you doubt it?" he asked.

" What ! " cried Hoffmann, " do I doubt it ? I should say so. I supped and waltzed with her last night."

" If that is so, it's an interesting case, and one to be noted in the annals of medicine. You will sign a statement of the facts, won't you ? "

" But I cannot sign, for I say that you lie. I say it is impossible; I say it is not so."

" Ah ! you say that it is not so," rejoined the doctor. " You say that to me, the physician to the prisons; to me, who did all that I could do to save her and failed; to me who bade her adieu when she mounted the tumbril ! You say that it is not so ! Wait ! "

Thereupon the doctor put out his hand, pressed a spring in the diamond clasp that held the velvet necklace in place, and removed the ribbon.

Hoffmann uttered a terrible cry. No longer supported by the only bond that attached it to the shoulders, the head fell from the bed to the floor, and did not stop until it touched Hoffmann's shoe, even as the brand had not stopped until it touched Arsène's foot.

The young man recoiled, and rushed down the stairs, shrieking, —

" I am mad ! "

There was no exaggeration in his exclamation. The slight partition separating sanity from insanity in the poet who exercises his cerebral faculties beyond measure, — that slight partition that sometimes seems ready to break, cracked in his brain with a noise like that made by a wall as it settles.

In those days people did not run far through the streets of Paris without telling why they were running. The Parisians had become very inquisitive in the year of grace 1793, and whenever a man was seen running, he was stopped in order that he might tell whom he was running after or who was running after him.

So it fell out that Hoffmann was stopped in front of the Church of the Assumption, which had been turned into a guard-house, and was taken before the commanding officer of the post.

There Hoffmann awoke to a realizing sense of the real danger of his position. Some took him for an aristocrat who had adopted that gait in order to reach the frontier more quickly. Others cried: "Down with the agent of Pitt and Coburg!" Some shouted: "To the nearest lamp-post!" which was not cheerful. Others: "To the Revolutionary Tribunal!" which was less cheerful still. People sometimes were saved from the lamp-post, witness Abbé Maury; but from the Revolutionary Tribunal, never!

Thereupon Hoffmann tried to explain what had happened to him since the previous evening. He told of his visit to the gambling-house and his winnings. He told how, with pockets filled with gold, he had hurried to Rue de Hanovre; how the woman he sought was no longer there; how, under the sway of the passion that consumed him, he had traversed the streets of Paris; how, as he crossed Place de la Révolution, he had found the woman he sought sitting at the foot of the guillotine; how she had taken him to a hotel in Rue Saint-Honoré, how they had danced and supped together, and how he had found, not a dead woman merely, but a headless woman, in the room that morning.

All this was very improbable, and Hoffmann's story gained little credence. The most fanatical partisans of truth called it a lie, the more moderate called it madness.

At this juncture one of those present conceived this method of throwing light on the question.

"You passed the night, you say, at a hotel on Rue Saint-Honoré?"

"Yes."

"You emptied your pockets, which were filled with gold, upon a table there?"

"Yes."

"You took supper there with the woman whose head, when it fell at your feet, caused the extraordinary terror under which you were laboring when we arrested you?"

"Yes."

"Very well! Let us look for the hotel. We probably shall not find the gold now, but we shall find the woman."

"Yes, yes," cried everybody. "Let us look for the hotel!"

Hoffmann would have been very glad not to go, but he had no choice but to obey the enthusiastic determination that followed the suggestion.

So he left the church and retraced his steps down Rue Saint-Honoré.

It was not a long distance from the Church of the Assumption to Rue Royale. And yet Hoffmann looked in vain, first carelessly, then with more attention, and at last with a very earnest desire to find what he sought. He saw nothing that reminded him of the hotel he had entered the night before, where he had passed the night, and which he had left a few moments before. Like the enchanted palaces that vanish when the stage-machinist has no further need of them, the hotel on Rue Saint-Honoré had utterly disappeared after the ghastly scene we have tried to describe had been played.

All this did not satisfy the fools who had accompanied

Hoffmann, and who were determined to reach some result that would compensate them for the trouble they had taken. Such a result could be attained only by the finding of Arsène's body or by the arrest of Hoffmann as a suspicious person.

As they failed to find Arséne's body, they were seriously discussing the advisability of arresting Hoffmann, when he suddenly spied the little man in black, and appealed to him for help, invoking his testimony to the truth of the story he had told.

The voice of a physician always has a great influence on the multitude. The little man mentioned his profession, and was allowed to approach Hoffmann.

"Ah! poor fellow!" he said, taking his hand on the pretext of feeling his pulse, but really to urge him, by a significant pressure, not to contradict what he said. "Poor fellow! so he has escaped!"

"Escaped from where? escaped from what?" cried twenty voices in chorus.

"Yes, escaped from where?" demanded Hoffmann, refusing to accept the means of salvation the doctor offered him, which he considered humiliating.

"*Parbleu!* from the hospital," said the doctor.

"From the hospital!" cried the crowd. "What hospital?"

"The insane hospital!"

"O doctor, doctor!" cried Hoffmann; "no jesting!"

"The poor devil," cried the doctor, apparently heedless of Hoffmann's interruption, "the poor devil has lost some woman that he loved on the scaffold, it seems."

"Oh! yes, yes," cried Hoffmann. "I did love her well, but not as I love Antonia."

" Poor boy ! " said several women who were standing by, and who began to feel compassion for Hoffmann.

" Yes, since then," continued the doctor, " he has been the victim of a terrible hallucination. He imagines that he is gambling. He imagines that he wins. When he has won, he imagines that he will be able to buy the woman he loves. He runs through the streets with his gold. He finds a woman at the foot of the guillotine and takes her to some superb palace, some magnificent hotel, where he passes the night drinking and singing and dancing with her; and after that he finds her dead. Is n't that what he told you ? "

" Yes, yes," cried the crowd, " word for word."

" Very good ! very good ! " said Hoffmann, with a gleaming eye. " Will you say that it 's not true, doctor, when you were the one who unfastened the diamond clasp that held the velvet necklace ? Oh ! I ought to have suspected something when I saw the champagne ooze from under the necklace, when I saw the burning wood fall on her bare foot, and that bare foot, that dead foot extinguish it instead of being burned by it."

" You see," said the doctor, with an expression of deep sympathy and in a sad voice, " his mad fit is coming on again."

" What 's that, my mad fit ! " cried Hoffmann. " Do you dare to say that it is not true ? You dare to say that I did not sup last night with Arsène who was guillotined yesterday ! You dare to say that her velvet necklace was n't the only thing that kept her head on her shoulders ! You dare to say that, when you unfastened the clasp and removed the velvet, the head did not fall on the carpet ! Nonsense, doctor, nonsense; you know very well that what I say is true."

"You are convinced now, my friends, are n't you?" said the doctor.

"Yes, yes," cried a score of voices in the crowd, and those who said nothing nodded their heads sadly in token of assent.

"Very well, then," said the doctor, "call a cab so that I can take him back."

"Back where?" cried Hoffmann. "Where do you propose to take me?"

"Where?" said the doctor; "why, to the madhouse that you have just escaped from, my good friend. *Morbleu!* let me do what I say," he added in an undertone, "or I won't answer for your safety. These people will think that you have been laughing at them, and they 'll tear you to pieces."

Hoffmann sighed and let his arms fall.

"There, you see," said the doctor, "now he 's as gentle as a lamb. The paroxysm has passed. There, my friend, there, there!" And the doctor pretended to soothe Hoffmann by patting him, as one soothes an excited horse or an angry dog.

Meanwhile a cab had been summoned and had driven up.

"Get in quickly," said the doctor to Hoffmann.

Hoffmann obeyed. He had exhausted all his strength in the struggle.

"To Bicêtre!" said the doctor aloud, as he entered the cab behind Hoffmann.

"Where do you want to be put down?" he asked the young man in an undertone.

"At the Palais-Égalité," said Hoffmann, almost inaudibly.

"Off you go, driver," cried the doctor.

Then he waved his hand to the crowd.

"Long live the doctor!" they cried.

The crowd, when it is under the sway of any passion, is always impelled to cry long live some one, or down with some one.

At the Palais-Égalité the doctor called to the driver to stop.

"Adieu, young man," he said, "and if you take my advice you will start for Germany at the earliest possible moment.   France is n't a good place for men with such imaginations as yours."

With that he pushed Hoffmann out of the cab, and Hoffmann, still dazed by what had happened, would have walked straight under the wheels of a wagon coming in the opposite direction, had not a young man who was passing darted forward and caught him in his arms, as the driver of the wagon, on his side, made an effort to stop his horses.

The cab went its way.

The two young men, he who had almost fallen, and he who had saved him, exclaimed in the same breath, —

"Hoffmann!"

"Werner!"

Observing his friend's prostration, Werner led him into the garden of the Palais-Royal.

Thereupon the memory of all that had recently taken place recurred to Hoffmann's mind more vividly than ever, and he remembered Antonia's locket, which he had pawned at the German money-changer's.

He exclaimed in dismay as he reflected that he had emptied all his pockets on the marble table at the hotel. But at the same instant he remembered that he had put three louis, with which to redeem the portrait, in his watch-pocket.

The pocket had loyally retained its treasure. The three louis were still there.

Hoffmann escaped from Werner's arms, crying, "Wait for me!" and hurried away in the direction of the money-changer's office.

At every step that he took it seemed to him as if he were emerging from a dense vapor, and advancing, through an ever-lightening cloud, toward a pure and resplendent atmosphere.

At the money-changer's door he paused to take breath. The old vision, the vision of the night had almost vanished.

Having recovered his breath he entered the shop.

The money-changer was in his place. The copper bowls were in their places.

At the noise made by Hoffmann in entering, the money-changer raised his head.

"Aha!" he said, "is it you, my young countryman? Faith! I confess that I did not expect to see you again."

"I trust that you don't say that because you have disposed of the locket!" cried Hoffmann.

"No, I promised you that I would keep it, and if I had been offered twenty-five louis for it instead of the three you owe me, the locket would not have left my shop."

"Here are the three louis," said Hoffmann, timidly. "But I confess that I am not able to pay you any interest."

"Interest for one night," said the money-changer, "nonsense, you are joking. Interest on three louis for one night, and from a fellow-countryman too! never!" And he handed him the locket.

"Thanks, mein herr," said Hoffmann. "And now."

he added, with a sigh, "I must go and try to get some money to take me back to Mannheim."

"To Mannheim," said the money-changer. "Tell me, are you of Mannheim?"

"No, I am not of Mannheim, but I live at Mannheim. My promised bride is at Mannheim. She is waiting for me, and I am going back to Mannheim to marry her."

"Aha!" said the money-changer; and as the young man had his hand on the door-knob he added, —

"I wonder if you know an old friend of mine at Mannheim, a musician?"

"Named Gottlieb Murr?" cried Hoffmann.

"The same! Do you know him?"

"Do I know him! I should say so, as his daughter is to be my wife."

"Antonia?" cried the money-changer. "What do you say, young man? that you were returning to Mannheim to marry Antonia?"

"To be sure."

"In that case remain in Paris, for you would take a fruitless journey."

"Why so?"

"Because here is a letter from her father telling me that Antonia died suddenly, as she was playing the harp, eight days ago, at three o'clock in the afternoon."

It was the very day that Hoffmann had gone to Arsène's house to paint her portrait. It was the very hour when he had pressed his lips to her bare shoulder.

Deathly pale, trembling, crushed, Hoffmann opened the locket in order to put Antonia's image to his lips, but the ivory was as white and spotless as if it had never been touched by the brush of the painter.

Nothing of Antonia was left to Hoffmann, twice false to his oath, not even the image of her to whom he had sworn everlasting love.

Two hours later Hoffmann, accompanied by Werner and the worthy broker, took his place in the diligence for Mannheim, where he arrived just in time to follow to the cemetery the body of old Gottlieb Murr, who had prayed on his death-bed to be buried beside his dear Antonia.

THE END.